The Three of Us

The Three of Us

Ore Agbaje-Williams

JONATHAN CAPE
LONDON

1 3 5 7 9 10 8 6 4 2

Jonathan Cape, an imprint of Vintage, is part of the Penguin
Random House group of companies whose addresses can be
found at global.penguinrandomhouse.com

Penguin
Random House
UK

First published by Jonathan Cape in 2023

penguin.co.uk/vintage

Set in 11.16/17 pt Palatino LT Pro
Typeset by Jouve (UK), Milton Keynes
Printed and bound in Great Britain by Clays Ltd, Elcograf S.p.A.

The authorised representative in the EEA is
Penguin Random House Ireland, Morrison Chambers,
32 Nassau Street, Dublin D02 YH68

A CIP catalogue record for this book is available
from the British Library

HB ISBN 9781787334083
TPB ISBN 9781787334335

Penguin Random House is committed to a sustainable future
for our business, our readers and our planet. This book is
made from Forest Stewardship Council® certified paper.

for Grace, duh

One

Temi comes over at twelve. She brings along the wine and the Kettle Chips I asked her to bring, as well as a packet of cigarettes. She called when she was at the till to ask if I needed a lighter, because the woman who was serving her had asked the same question. I could tell she had the phone in between her shoulder and her chin because I could hear her coat rustling. I said no to the lighter, because we had matches at home, but also because I knew I wouldn't end up smoking, not if my husband would be able to smell it on me.

She was late, I knew she would be. She told me she would get here by eleven but it was eleven forty-five when she called me from the shop. I knew she would be late before that, though, because she always is. It's her thing. She's the only person I let come to anything late. That's what happens when you're best friends. You let things slide. Besides, today we were supposed to have been in another country, acting like we didn't speak English and wearing sunglasses indoors, and it's my fault we're not – something that she reminded me of when she informed me this morning that she would be coming over. I haven't seen her in almost a month so I can't really justify complaining. So anyway, she arrives at twelve. She gets out of the car mid-story, like she'd started telling it the moment she saw me approaching from the front door and just thought I'd pick up what I'd missed as she told the rest of it. She was talking about someone, I didn't know who.

It was someone who'd been sending her links to cat videos on YouTube. She said she didn't even know people still watched cat videos on YouTube, and I agreed, I thought we'd moved on to TikTok and Instagram for stuff like that. Anyway, she continued, I asked him to stop. I said, When have you ever known me to be a cat person? By then we've moved into the house, hugged, and she's kicked off her shoes at the front door. We go to the kitchen and open the wine, and she does what she usually does, downs one glass first and then slowly sips the next. I don't ask if she is planning to sober up and drive home later because I assume she'll be leaving her car and calling an Uber like she always does.

He said he thought the videos were funny, that I would like them because they're funny videos, that I don't need to like cats in order to enjoy them. I eat the Kettle Chips as she talks, letting them soften a little on my tongue before I chew them because the crunch will get in the way of me hearing what Temi is saying, and she hates repeating herself.

I know that. I watched the videos, she says. They're quite funny. And since we won't be doing *cómo se dice* I'm seeing him on Tuesday. I have to clarify which person this is. She's seeing a few different guys and she gives them nicknames rather than calling them by their real names. If I tell you their names you'll get attached, she says. There's No Homo, who at dinner complimented a waiter's cufflinks and followed it by saying No Homo and then laughing, by himself, but who Temi finds funny even though she is laughing at him and not with him. Then there's TTM (Talk Too Much), the one who provides sad and lengthy monologues whenever Temi asks him a simple question like Where's your shirt from? or Would you like to share a starter? She only went out with him twice. After things fizzled out she messaged to ask him the name of the restaurant they'd been to and he sent her four paragraphs. So now they text platonically and she sends me the screenshots. Maybe we'll read through the new ones later. There's also Woman, so called because she discovered that's how he referred to her amongst his friends. She was tricked into meeting them on their second date when he invited her to have a picnic in the park but neglected to mention that his friends and family would be there. It was his birthday party.

This one, though, she's not told me about before – or at least I don't remember him. I did, she says when I tell her he doesn't ring a bell. She uses her arm to demonstrate how tall he is (about a foot taller than she is, apparently) and puts her hand between her legs and knocks her knees together, hops from foot to foot. Oh. It all comes back to me. Desperate For The Loo? Yes! See I knew you'd remember. She swivels the packet of crisps towards herself. Now, I don't think he's boyfriend material, which is a problem, because of course I have the weddings coming up, so I need to keep him within striking distance, you know? I nod, take a large swig of wine and try the wine-tasting thing my husband was showing me on his phone the other day. Speaking of which, Temi says, where's yours?

*

I met Temi when I was eleven. We were at the same secondary school, although by Year 10 she'd moved up a year, that's how intelligent she is. We both had the big rucksacks, the fresh braids with no colour because our school was strict about that, even though the white girls who went to the Caribbean on their summer holidays were allowed a single limp braid with coloured thread in it.

Temi accidentally bumped into me when we were getting changed after PE, and my deodorant slipped out of my hand and on to the floor. I picked it up and there was hair and some other unknown material stuck to it. It was organic because my mother had recently read about the link between deodorant and cancer somewhere and made my sisters and me throw away our old ones. The organic ones were seven pounds each and I knew she'd be angry if I came home and told her it was ruined. Temi grimaced as she peered over my shoulder to see what she'd done. Sorry yeah, she said, maybe just rinse it in the sink and it will come off? Even though it was an idiotic solution (because I was never going to let anything that had touched the floor anywhere near my body again), I appreciated the attempt at one, and said thanks. I was the last to leave the changing room because I wanted to sniff my armpits in peace to see what the damage was and she came back in to look for something just as I was doing it. She laughed and fished a spray deodorant out of her rucksack and held it out to me. It was the first time someone persuaded me to do something I had been told was wrong. Obviously that was the most innocent 'bad' thing I could have done at that age. But when you have the fear of your mother guiding you, there isn't a lot you're willing to do in the first place. After that we very naturally became friends. We ate lunch together, texted each other every day with the little credit we were allowed, studied for tests and exams together, and even our mothers became friends in a way, trading tips for how to talk your way out of a parking ticket and cursing about our fathers in Yoruba when they thought we couldn't understand. There are a few years between my sisters and me, and we have never been close. But Temi and me, we spent a lot of time together during those years, and we've been best friends ever since.

She is probably the only person in my life who has never wanted something from me, only for me.

*

I turn to the cupboards to get a bowl and pour half of the Kettle Chips into it. He's where you think he is, I say, and she rolls her eyes. That man is a workaholic, I'm telling you. I did tell you. He never takes a day off. It's always work, work, work. You know you're in a throuple, right? she says. A what? I ask. A throuple, she repeats, annoyed. It's when three people are in a relationship together. In your case, the third person is his job. I've never met anyone who works as much he does. When's the last time he took a day off? What was the point of cancelling our holiday if he was just going to be at work the whole time? I thought you said he wanted you guys to spend more time together? And yet the other day didn't you tell me he's been coming home past eight most days? It's both impressive and terrifying. I thought I worked hard – she scoffs – I thought *you* worked hard to pretend to remain interested in him, but this man, this man is truly something special. How does he expect to make a baby with you if he's never at home? I take a large gulp of my wine and swish it around in my cheeks like it's Listerine. It's a contentious subject, the baby thing. When I told her we were going to start trying for one she thought I was having some kind of crisis. Then she disappeared to Lagos for a month and I took that as a sign she didn't want to talk about it any more.

The truth is that I don't want children. Or I have never actively considered the reality of having them. I am not maternal, and am unconvinced that I've witnessed parenting that is good enough to replicate. I can even admit that I'm a little selfish. I like to remain in control, and children – babies – do not allow for that. But over time my husband has convinced me – or I've let him, and a recent (and deeply uncomfortable) conversation with his mother, who is nice but very much believes that the world revolves around her son – that we should at least try for one child. I'd sat across from her in her house and listened to her explain that it is our duty as children to continue the family line, the family name, by building our own and honouring our parents with grandchildren. That my desire to wait was self-serving, and that I should remember that it's not all about me. She used her eyes to guide my gaze towards my husband, then back to herself and said to me, Your parents must have told you this now? I looked again at my husband – who was in silent but clear agreement with his mother – then at my mother-in-law, and nodded slowly. She nodded back, and that was the end of the discussion. Now whenever she sees me, not pregnant, she frowns.

Temi and I used to argue with other people about how children are the worst kind of pollution, that really if we wanted to help the planet we should kill half of the population, then ourselves, and use the remains as compost for planting trees. That was after watching a strangely intense documentary in Geography, but even though the mass-suicide idea faded away, the no-children sentiment remained – sort of. Yet one brief conversation with my mother-in-law during which I could see my husband daydreaming about holding a baby as I lay sweating in a hospital bed later, I was apparently trying for a baby. I stopped taking birth control. I was swallowing daily vitamins and avoiding drinking coffee. I was weirdly proud of myself for it, even though the period pains I've experienced in the last three months have been more than any human should bear. But amidst all this, my husband got promoted – yay for him and everything – and now he's just never home, ever. It's difficult to have a baby with someone who is never around. I mostly only see him in the middle of the night, when I get up to snack or wee.

This morning we craned our necks over the sink to look as only one line appeared on the test. I went to pick it up and he stopped my hand by holding his in the way. It says you need to wait at least fifteen minutes, he said. I'm aware – it's been almost seven. So then we need to wait the next eight minutes out. You're going to be late, and another line won't show up in eight minutes. He looked at me for a second then looked back to the test, like he was about to miss the miraculous arrival of the line. Why are you so sure? Because this is the sixth test I've taken in three months and nothing ever changes after the first three minutes. He pinched at the bottom of his nose and left the room, then I heard the front door open and close. I waited a minute – for him to come back and say he'd left his phone or his car key – and lifted the test and squinted at it. Then I pressed the pedal on the bin, dropped the test inside and washed my hands.

I'm not even convinced he still wants kids, I eventually respond to Temi, who has been watching me. Look, sis, she says, leaning over the kitchen counter to touch my arm, you've never wanted them anyway. I say bin the whole thing and get an IUD. I laugh because she does and then she takes her hand away, swallows a large amount of wine, lifts her glass off the counter, stands up. Anyway, baby talk is boring. She walks out of the kitchen and into the hallway, then comes back for the bag of crisps. How's the remodel going?

We've been remodelling the upstairs bathrooms and library for the last year. I don't mean just redecorating, I mean changing the whole shape and structure. They were perfectly fine before – even my mother, who is notoriously judgemental of anything I do that has not required her input, said our home was a 'nice' place. And yet last year my husband decided that he wanted to rip the whole thing apart. He didn't explain why exactly, but he was adamant about it. I tend not to be concerned about these things, and I didn't think it would take very long. But we've been remodelling the same three rooms for a year now and we've had to use the downstairs bathroom for the entire time. I know I sound spoiled. Oh we have three bathrooms and I have to use the downstairs one, but we have a lot of stairs, and it's a long way to travel for a shower or a poo.

I take Temi upstairs and point at the drawings pinned to the walls in each room, the paint samples dotted around and the Thermos in the corner of one of the bathrooms that has been there for a year because a contractor we tried out left it behind. I lead her into the library where the floor is covered with something like a see-through tarpaulin and it makes an irritating noise as we walk across it to get to the window that's just been installed. You didn't win on the window, huh? Temi asks. I shake my head no and look at it again. It's one large single window that goes across the entire back wall of the library. It's the only thing that my husband has decided on and not changed his mind about in the past year. We actually argued about it – and normally I wouldn't have minded – but the idea of the window was so garish to me, I don't know why anyone would need a whole wall as a window. He said that it was elegant and stylish, and I said it would make the room cold. He said we had heated flooring and I said we shouldn't be spending extra money every month to heat a room that is cold because of a wall-sized window. His response was to smile and say, I don't think we're really people who need to be concerned about money, are we? Eventually, I realised that I didn't care enough to press the issue, and let him have it.

Now you need a maid, Temi says as we look below us at the half-done patio. Why? I ask. Because then we would have hot chocolates to warm us in this bloody freezing room.

*

Temi wouldn't call herself rich but she is. Her father works for an oil company and her mother is a GP. Then of course her mother's father is one of the largest shareholders at the company where her father works. Her father earned the job he has, though – she made a point of telling me that when she explained that she was not rich, even though she is. The first time I went to her house, the maid, who was white English and wearing one of those black and white uniforms that I haven't seen on anyone else since I watched *Princess Diaries 2*, said 'Hello, Miss' and took my coat at the door and then asked what I wanted to eat and drink. She stood and waited for my answer, but the uniform looked so comical, and the house girls I'd seen in Nigeria wore their own clothes, so I thought it was some kind of weird joke, and eventually Temi answered for both of us. Then there's the actual house – it's big, like big-big. At the time I didn't even know houses like that existed – I do now, because I live in one – but back then I had to subtly pop my eyes back inside my head and pretend it was perfectly normal.

It wasn't like a show home either, where everything looks like no one lives there and the furniture is being rented by the hour. They had 'family' photos, a disproportionate number of which only featured Temi's two older brothers; there were board games in the living room and a half-finished jigsaw puzzle on one of the long, grand dining tables. They had a fridge with various wedding invitations on it, messages written with those magnet letters no one really has any more. They even had a chalkboard wall where someone had written 'House Shopping List' in a beautiful cursive. Temi showed me her room, with its posters and bookshelves, and clothes all over the floor. She showed me her parents' separate studies, the reading room, and then she took me into the kitchen where the maid had prepared two hot chocolates and grilled cheese sandwiches, each with a small side salad.

I wasn't poor, but I wasn't rich either, and everything about Temi fascinated me. She didn't flaunt her wealth but she never pretended it didn't exist. She didn't care when the other Nigerian girls in our school claimed she wasn't Nigerian enough because she had only been to Nigeria once. We were two of maybe thirty Black girls at a grammar school whose architecture was desperate to communicate that it was teetering on the edge of being private. We were sister to a boys' school which was a stone's throw away across the field we shared. Our school specialised in mathematics and science and regularly achieved the best GCSE and A-level results in the county. Parents sent their children there because they expected them to excel. The evenings after school were packed with extracurricular activities designed to prep us for personal statements that would make us look interesting and academically desirable.

People who attended our school were generally financially comfortable but few were as rich as Temi and her family. But one of the first things I realised about her was that she didn't fit the profile of rich, smart girl from rich, smart family that I would have expected. She had an impeccable academic record, yes – our school made all grades public, and only once did Temi, who rarely studied, mostly just flicked through textbooks like they were magazines, not top the class, an instance in which she was joint first with a girl who'd studied for eight hours straight all week – but she wasn't quietly formidable. She did everything out loud. She disagreed with teachers in front of the class, she wore her uniform however she wanted to, she switched subjects at GCSE without her parents' knowledge because she knew that she didn't want to study medicine like her brothers, and she was sick of them trying to manage her life. She didn't care when people said she should stop showing off because she knew the answers to everything, or when a girl in our class started dating one of her brothers. That was Year 9, and she accurately predicted that her brother would end it within six weeks. I'd never met someone my age who already knew who she was and didn't shape herself around other people's opinions.

She was the complete opposite of me – being moulded in every possible way by my parents, who had written out their expectations on biblical stone tablets the day I was conceived. Parents who expected me back from school punctually every day, as though they were being charged for every minute I was late. Parents who studied my report cards for errors and inconsistencies to later deduct from my monthly allowance. Our backgrounds were similar, but where Temi got her confidence from, I have never been able to understand. While Temi had worked out what else was possible beyond her parents' plans for her, I looked to mine to tell me what to do. It wasn't what I wanted, but to obey was better than to defy without knowledge of the alternative. My parents wanted perfection without complaint. They believed they were raising three perfect wives, mothers, professionals. They wanted to play a game of my horse is bigger than yours with every parent in the country and win every time. Temi always wanted (and still wants) to show me things – things I'd never seen or experienced before, places I'd never been, people I'd never encountered, ways of being that had never occurred to me – to show me that I was capable of so much more. Your parents don't want you to be great, she would say, they want you to be like everyone else.

Until Temi, I didn't know it was even possible to decide things for myself. Becoming friends with Temi was like having someone lift the lid on my sheltered life and offer a hand to pull me out.

*

My husband calls just as we walk into our bedroom so that I can show Temi some of the new things I bought for the holiday we're not on. He rarely calls me when he's at work, so I start by asking who died. What? No one. I'm just tired, it's just not been a good day. Are you cooking later? Temi mouths who is it and I gesture at my engagement and wedding rings with my right pinkie. You're the only one who uses the pots in this house, I say, and he says, Okay, can we get a takeaway? We run through options: Chinese, Indian, Japanese, Italian, Thai. Temi says, Oooh Thai, and I hear my husband sigh. When did she get back? A few days ago, I say, wondering how long he will wait until after she leaves to ask how long *I* was going to wait to tell him that. Is she staying for dinner? he asks. By this point I have put the phone on speaker. It's possible I do this on purpose. I'm staying forever! Temi says as she leans towards the phone, her wine glass against her chest. My husband suggests Japanese food, and then says that he'll find a place and send a menu, that I should tell him what I want and he'll order it, pick it up on his way home. He hangs up and texts immediately to say that if Temi has decided to infiltrate our evening then she will need to reimburse him for her food.

In my wardrobe, Temi pulls out items and tries to guess which ones my husband chose and which ones I did. My husband has a peculiar sartorial taste when it comes to me, like he's imagined that he married someone from Stepford when he married someone from Enfield. I've never told him that I don't like the things he buys me, because sometimes when we decide to spice things up I put them on and he likes it. I don't wear them outside the house, though. I have some semblance of pride.

There's a silk skirt I bought a few months back that Temi picks out and asks where exactly I plan on wearing it. You never go out any more, she says, and she's not wrong, but I shop regardless. It's something my mother hates about me. You have a degree and no job. A house but no children. You're like an empty fridge. Expensive to run and yet completely useless. My choice not to work, among others, is a reason my mother and I have a difficult relationship.

Whenever she calls – at least twice a week, usually on Monday mornings to berate me again for not working, or Friday evenings to interrupt whatever social plans I have and berate me for not spending time with my husband or being pregnant – she finds ways of pointing out the exceptional things that my two sisters have accomplished and are currently doing. My oldest sister, who is married to a heart surgeon and has three children, is a biochemical engineer who lives in a wealthy part of Dulwich. My other sister, who is two years older than me, is married to a financial analyst, pregnant with her second child and also a partner at a law firm where the annual revenue is nine figures.

My mother usually opens her phone calls with a professional success story of one of my sisters followed by something one of their children has done, like walking or speaking. Accolades that neither of us will remember the moment the phone call is over. She wants to make a point, a statement that I am not achieving the things that they are, and therefore I am falling behind. But her parameters of success are constantly changing, and it's impossible to catch or keep up.

Temi's ideas have always been more radical than mine. After she realised that her gender would always make her secondary to her brothers in her parents' eyes, she developed a burn-it-all-down-and-start-over approach. I only attempted change at university because Temi had been insistent that I make the most of my freedom once I got there. I found the concept of it – no guidelines, no consistent structure – unsettling. I didn't understand how to 'be' without my parents around, or without Temi there to answer all my questions about everything. When I got to university, it took a while for me to know exactly how to take advantage of my new situation. I started off by trying to disappear, making myself invisible to everyone. I thought that if I got too close to anyone, I'd end up morphing into them. After my first term I thought I'd been successful. I'd made arm's-length friends: people I would say hello to if we happened to bump into each other, people I could exchange seasonal text messages with, but didn't have to worry about receiving a birthday text from, or a message just 'checking in'. No expectations.

Then I caught up with Temi over Christmas drinks and she talked about the life she'd built for herself at university: different groups of friends for different occasions, stories of nights out, stories of men she'd humiliated, etc. I wasn't surprised – Temi is good at carving out her own spaces and creating the reality she wants – but I was jealous. No one expected anything from me but no one knew me either. Temi watched me tilt my head from side to side, stir my drink with a straw and sigh at every anecdote, and eventually said, So what is your problem today? I explained: I didn't understand what to do with all this space away from my parents. First, she laughed. When she'd stopped laughing she looked at me and asked if I was being serious. Finally, she rolled her eyes at me and spoke between sips of her rosé: Look. Like I've always said – it's your life. You do you. But this is sad. You get messages from +44 numbers and not in a fun way. You spend most evenings in your room? What is that? What kind of disturbing things will I find if I go through your internet history? You're wasting precious time. You're going to pick up your degree and walk straight back into your parents' house. Maybe that's what you want – but even if you do, wouldn't you want to have made the most of *this* time? Start an argument, miss a deadline, tell some lies. Whatever you want to do. Just don't stay at university for three years sitting inside your room. You're Black, sure, but you can still get jaundice.

A few weeks after Temi's sermon, I figured out – eventually – how to enjoy myself. I learned to create a reality that suited my mood depending on what it was that day.

I dated men who believed me when I said I was a model studying on the side to keep my mind fresh, or an international student from Seville whose au pair had been English, or a stressed medical student who really needed to bum a cigarette to relax before her final exams. I submitted blank documents to professors and claimed the file must have been corrupted. I stole Samantha's vegan sausages and feigned ignorance while she fought with Clarence and the non-English-speaking student about who had stolen them. I wore clothes that would have made my mother disown me. I never paid for a taxi on a night out. I woke up every morning and chose violence. I woke up every morning and chose myself, before everyone else, no matter the consequences. Sometimes it felt like I'd left my body behind and had let my mind inhabit a new one.

And it was fun while it lasted. But I wasn't like Temi and none of it came naturally to me. I wanted a freedom that was quiet and contained. I began to realise that control was the only thing that I had never been given and really wanted. Being married to my husband provides that for me now. I am in control of who I am to him and he sees what I want him to see. Marriage, with its lifelong social and economic security, ticks off at least one thing on my parents' list of expectations. It might not look like what Temi expected when she told me to do whatever I wanted to do but it has created a balance in which I have liberated myself from my parents as long as I'm married. It works perfectly.

Nonetheless Temi still doesn't understand my relationship with my husband, how it even exists. Why him though, she often says, usually whilst chewing something, an elbow on the table, forearm raised and wrist hanging, like she's so irked she can't be bothered to lift it.

*

Temi tries on the silk skirt and she doesn't look as good in it as I do. Because I'm at home all the time, it means I have more opportunities to exercise. My husband bought me a Peloton bike and hired a personal trainer who comes to the house on Wednesdays and Saturdays. We do cardio and HIIT, and some Pilates, some yoga. I've never been more toned, and I can eat whatever I want. Temi doesn't have the bum to pull off the skirt, it just kind of hangs off her and I tell her. She kisses her teeth at me and says I know, you stole my butt, that's why yours is so big.

She asks to see the new dress, the one I texted her about a few weeks ago while she was away. My husband has a work function coming up, one of those where people bring their spouses and try to figure out who has been lying about how attractive theirs is. I've been to two before and they're actually quite entertaining. At the first one, my husband was still quite junior so no one was really paying attention to us apart from his boss's wife, who kept touching my braids while asking if she could touch my braids. D'you mind, she said, rubbing the ends of them between her fingers. Then, Can you feel it when I do this? she said while pulling. No, no not at all, I said, smiling, and lifted the braid out of her hand. Fascinating, she said, then winked at me. By the time the second event came around my husband had been promoted and people shook his hand as we walked in, nodded and smiled, raised half-empty glasses of alcohol. People bothered to ask my name and he introduced me as his better half. We discussed it later in the car home because I told him he sounded Caucasian when he did that and he found that insulting, then I called him racist and he didn't like that either. His boss's wife had been replaced by a different woman, who was Indian and had a slit going up the leg of her dress. She and I became allies, and she let me have a few cigarettes when she found me outside getting some 'fresh air'. I told her about the previous wife and she laughed, then told me a similar story about the boss, about how he'd asked her to wear a Native American head tie and that she'd had to explain that she wasn't Native American. He'd said, I thought all Indians were Indians – a poor attempt at an apology. It's fine, though, she said while blowing out smoke, we split up last week. I came tonight as a favour.

I pull out the dress: it's long and a deep red colour, with a slit up the front. If I'm honest, I took a mental photo of the boss's second ex-wife's dress that night and searched for three days straight to find it online. I knew I would look better in it. Temi takes it out of my hands and laughs. Are you serious? You're going to make your poor tasteless husband drool. Drooooooool. Her phone rings then and she walks over to the mirror and puts the dress in front of herself as she picks up the call. For what? she says. No, Samuel. Yeah, Adam, that's what I said. Whatever, forget it. You are single now, okay? Yes I have been drinking, why, haven't you? Oh come on, you were so drunk that you fell asleep at the restaurant! I left you there because my Uber was outside? Yeah yeah okay I could have woken you up but those late charges add up, you know. My signal is bad blah blah. She hangs up, and finds me pretending to look at the clothes in my wardrobe like I've never seen them before. Ask me, she says. I shrug comedically, as though I don't know what she's talking about. Ask me, she says again, looking at herself in the mirror with the dress held up against her body. Okay, I say – how could you leave a drunk man asleep at a restaurant on a date and not tell me? She laughs as she puts the dress back. Honestly? It was so embarrassing. He was actually intelligent, he might have even been as good-looking as me, but he drank like a fish. She shakes her head as I laugh, and then it dawns on me. Temi doesn't go Dutch. Who paid? She drags her eyes from my clothes to me, low and irritated, then draws them back to the clothes again. I don't think you understand, he drank a lot. Like five glasses of wine and two beers. And he even tried some of my cocktail. Then he had the audacity to say I should have woken him up! The only thing I should have done is send him an invoice! That restaurant had three Michelin stars and he had been bragging about how much money he made so I ordered the Dover sole! I never should have even picked up his call. When a woman ghosts you after a few dates, you have to get – the – message. She pinches two of her fingers together as she says it. I like seeing her excitable like this – I know that she actually enjoys when dates go badly because then it means she has a story to tell me. When even was this date? Like three days ago. She has clearly been saving this story. So wait, why did he call *today*? Oh! she says, turning to face me as she walks over and puts the dress back – he wanted *me* to apologise. Imagine it takes you three days to pluck up small-small courage to call me and it's to ask me to say sorry. And I was like – for what, Adam? For what? She shakes her head. Hold on, I say, so you do know what his name is. Yeah. So why did you call him Samuel? Ha, she says, running her hands along the sleeve of one of my old jumpers. Then she walks back to the middle of the room where her wine glass is and sips from it, smiling at me.

Sometimes I get jealous listening to her stories. They are full of chaos and one-liners and people who seem cartoonish and contrived but are somehow real. Whenever she tells them – always with a drink in hand – I am completely rapt. She says that I look like I wish I was her, and sometimes I wish I was, even if just to have the stories to tell, and the ability to still live a life that meant I experienced them. Back at university when I used to date like Temi, for light entertainment, we used to compare bad dates, sending ratings and one-word reviews to each other. T&S, as in Trinny and Susannah, was the phrase used to describe a man who had clearly dressed in the dark. David, or Goliath, was for men who were either a lot smaller or a lot larger than the available pictures of them we found on Facebook suggested. Magician was for men who wore black turtle necks with black blazers and looked like they might pull a dove or an endless line of tied handkerchiefs out of their pockets. My favourite was probably RRR (Reduce, Reuse, Recycle): men who were incredibly pleasing to look at but spoke purely in phrases used by footballers in post-match interviews, like 'At the end of the day', or 'We got the job done out there tonight', or the most commonly used phrase that Temi and I would hear at the end of a date when we were saying goodnight but the man thought things were going well and that we should get a drink elsewhere: 'It's early doors.'

We used to dedicate entire lunch dates to swapping stories, but now I sit and listen to hers instead. The last stories I told her were about my husband, when we had just started dating. Of course he didn't put his tongue down my throat when he first kissed me, but he tried later, on the third date. There were some texts he sent me that were embarrassing to receive, let alone for him to have written and decided to send. Once, he arrived half an hour early to pick me up for a date and was irritated when I wasn't ready. I was napping, I told Temi when we were on Skype the next day, and she spluttered, some of the water she was drinking splashing on to the lens of her laptop camera. She wiped it off with the sleeve of her jumper and covered her mouth as she laughed. You were napping? Yes! I was tired. He called me just as I was hitting the sweet spot in my nap. But when were you going to get ready? she said. When I woke up. And when were you going to wake up? I don't know, maybe when he arrived. She laughed. And he looks like the type to wait too. Then she said that honestly men are as stupid as the heterosexual monogamy that forces us to be with them. It was one of those things she said as a passing comment, but I still thought about it afterwards, like I thought about everything she said. Between the two of us she was the one who had the street smarts, who knew what men were like because of her brothers, the various men she dated and the men she turned down. Until the day I got married I had doubts about the relationship because I knew Temi didn't fully approve. She didn't understand how I had gone from laughing at him with her, to taking his last name. Even though we've now been married for three years Temi still questions me, him, the whole thing. Some of her questions I have answers to, but others sit in the back of my mind, reappearing just when I think I have everything under control.

*

It takes about an hour for the alcohol to really set in for Temi, and I can tell because she starts making little jokes about my husband's clothes, pulls at the sleeves of some of his shirts and blazers and kisses her teeth, says that ten years ago I would have spat out my Sauvignon Blanc at a man who dressed like him. When she turns to me and says, You've changed, you know, I can tell that she's feeling relaxed. We move over from my wardrobe to the bedroom. Temi makes a point of telling me that she likes this time we spend together, just the two of us, that it feels like old times, and that's when I can really tell that the alcohol

is getting to her. She is not one to romanticise or be nostal-
gic or loving about anything.

There are piles of books and photo albums around, things
that would normally go in the library, but because it's being
forever remodelled, they are either stacked in our room or
in the garage. Temi asks me to grab the bottle of wine from
downstairs, which I do, and when I get back she's picked up
two photo albums and taken them over to the bed, where she
sits cross-legged, slowly looking through one of them while
her wine glass sits empty in her hand. I take it from her and
fill it up, then mine, and sit next to her on the bed. There
are photos from my wedding, of me with various family
members, with friends from university, with children of old
work friends of my parents, who my parents had insisted be
invited. Photos of Temi and my sister-in-law. They almost
look like they're in love. In every picture they're laughing
or smiling, fixing one another's hair or dress or make-up. I
remember on the way to the wedding asking which of them
would be fixing my train during the ceremony and hearing them sniggering in the back of the car. Later they asked
the photographer for a photo together, a photo without me.
Temi points at it now and says, Remember, you were really
jealous that day. Could have killed us both. I smile and sip,
reach over to turn the page. There are portraits of my husband and me, taken by the water on the edge of the private
estate where we got married. We spent about an hour taking

photos, just us and the photographer. In almost every photo, my husband is looking at me, and I'm looking away. When Temi first saw them she said they looked like an advert for Sandals, that resort company. Like we were being paid to look like a couple and it was the first time we'd met. It's easier for me to laugh about it now, but at the time I thought the photos were amazing, that we looked like the most attractive people to have ever existed. Temi taps at one photo in which I am finally looking at my husband at the same time as he's looking at me. I can't even believe I'm saying this, Temi says, but it really seems like you like him here, you know, like maybe you actually are in love with this person. I'm shocked and I think you deserve an Oscar. She takes a significant gulp of wine.

It's been an ongoing theme throughout my relationship with my husband, that Temi believes that I don't love him, and that I have a brilliant endgame that I am working towards. It started the day she paid me a surprise visit in my third year at university. My husband was with me at my flat and while he was in the bathroom, she turned to me and said, Okay, tell me, what is it, what's the prank? I was genuinely confused, and asked her what she was talking about, and, as he returned to the room, she whispered, It's fine, tell me later. We spent the rest of the day together – the three of us – sat on the sofa, me sitting in between them, watching old episodes of *One on One* and *My Family* and passing glasses to whoever was closest to a bottle of wine for refills. At one point, when Temi had gone to the toilet, my husband looked at his watch and asked when she was going to leave and I'd shrugged. Just before nine he sighed and coughed a few times and Temi continued to watch the TV, unperturbed. By ten he had increased the frequency of his coughing and sighing and Temi went to the kitchen and returned with a glass of water. Here. You're coughing at all the funny parts and it's annoying, no one likes having to rewind. And if you have the plague please consult the doctor about your weak immune system, maybe he can fix your hairline too. He put the water down and said, I'm not ill. I'm just wondering when you're going to leave. Oh, she said, as she rearranged the cushions around herself – I was literally thinking the same thing about you. He waited another half hour then relented and went home. At the door he told me quietly that he'd see me the next day. Temi craned her neck to watch him leave and once the door had closed she turned her whole body to me, white wine spritzer in hand, and said, Honestly, if you tell me it's a big prank, I'll respect you so much, like honestly, but otherwise I think maybe you're playing a prank on yourself, 'cause this guy – she pointed towards the front door – I mean . . . sis. Be serious.

Then I got engaged, and I sent Temi a picture of me wearing the ring, smiling, my husband behind me, and she called me a few moments later. Yeah so I'm confused about where the endgame is here. I thought this was like a guy for events and stuff. You know if you go through with this you'll probably have to take his last name, right? You know that he's going to tell you what to wear, who to talk to, what to say, when to arrive, when to leave, how to sit, how to stand, like control your whole life the way your parents did. I remember us saying we weren't even doing the marriage thing, that we would shock our parents by walking around saying *my partner* and daring them to freak out about what exactly we meant. That if we ever decided to do this, like throw our freedom away for the ring and the wedding like our mothers did, that we'd at least do it with someone who we could be ourselves with. I get the whole opposites-attract thing but you are not even remotely compatible. When you're around him you barely speak. You're not you.

I took a few seconds to think about what she had said. Look, she continued, all I'm saying is, this man doesn't fit into the plans we made. We said no more parents controlling our lives, but this isn't it. It's a nice ring, for sure, someone who has taste probably helped him to pick it out, but you can keep the ring and not spend the rest of your life with him, you know? We can find that unlucky idiot together. Go on the apps or whatever, find your one true love and do the fairytale-wedding thing if you must. It doesn't have to be all, oh look the human personification of A4 ruled paper, let me tether myself to him for life.

But my husband and I match because he expects nothing from me. At university I was experimenting, trying to work out who I was, what I wanted from life. The need to constantly reinvent myself became tiresome and nothing felt comfortable, or close enough to who I was still unsure I was. I dated people but they still wanted things from me, expected certain behaviour. So when my husband and I went on our first date and he talked about his hopes for a life without complication, it was refreshing. He wanted someone calm and beautiful, someone who would allow him to be the breadwinner, take care of finances and make all the important decisions. From the other person he wanted almost nothing. In my husband I found someone for whom the bare minimum was more than enough, someone who didn't expect anything of me that I wasn't willing to give. Temi doesn't see it this way, but being with my husband means security and acceptance without condition.

Occasionally I think back to the exhaustive lecture Temi gave when I got engaged and wonder if I do just like having someone around, but then I remember that even though I find his chewing too loud, and his little earring obnoxious, I do, in fact, love my husband. I love him because he loves me without requirement. His affection comes regardless of my level of enthusiasm on any given day, or my level of interest in his work or hobbies. I love him because his love isn't transactional, something I grew up believing was impossible for and inaccessible to me. And although our feelings for each other are different, I know that two different kinds of love can coexist. That I love him enough to have learned what affectionate couples do and have practised it enough to make him happy. He doesn't ask for it, but I have seen the way he looks at other couples engaging in frankly unethical public displays of affection and heard the way he talks about the other couples he knows and how they interact with each other, and realised that if nothing else, this is something just outside of my comfort zone that I can provide without complaint. And he loves me more for it. For my affection, for my calm, unbothered nature, for the unadulterated woman – blank by choice – that I am. It may sound like a role and maybe in a way it is, but it's one that doesn't involve any acting. In fact it barely involves any effort at all. And yes, the issue of children, and his expectation of them, has introduced a more complex layer to our relationship. But for now, it works.

*

Ten minutes later Temi and I get bored of flicking through the photo albums and move back downstairs. We're looking for snacks – we've finished the Kettle Chips. My husband and I have recently started a keto diet, something about long life and health, even though both of us are perfectly fit. It's also something to do with improving fertility apparently, although included in that is not drinking, so I make a mental note to hide the empty wine bottle somewhere in the guest room, and to wash, dry and replace the wine glasses, all before my husband gets home. It's almost half one now, and after rifling through the cupboards for a few minutes Temi finds two Snickers bars inside the empty bread tin and hands me one. They're my husband's. I know that because a) they're not mine and b) I've been eating and replacing them every week since we started this keto diet. I eat them downstairs in the middle of the night when I come down to use the toilet. After finishing my Snickers bar I sit and drink the last of the wine in my glass while Temi goes back to the cupboards for something else to eat, dissatisfied. Every time she spots something she finds interesting, she gasps, like she hasn't been to this house more than a hundred times before.

In the cupboard above the farmhouse sink, she picks out a packet of shallots and some extra virgin olive oil. You cook now? she says, holding each in a hand. Of course not, the packet is unopened, and the seal is still on the oil, see? I'm learning so much about you, she says, moving to the next cupboard, where she picks out two glasses with 'Mr' written on one and 'Mrs' written on the other. They're glasses my husband and I were gifted when we got married. They have glitter and sparkles on them and we are grown adults so we don't use them, but the person who gave them to us is apparently a close family friend on my father's side so we've kept them just in case they ever come over. Even though they live in Nigeria and didn't even come to the traditional wedding, let alone the white wedding. Temi holds one up in each hand and turns them over, mouthing 'Mr' and 'Mrs' a few times before letting her wrists drop slightly and looking at me. These remind me of your parents, you know, she says, and I'm wondering if she's going to get angry or cry, because sometimes she can be a bit of an emotional drunk, even though she's probably just tipsy, not quite drunk yet. But I also know that my parents are a sore subject for both of us.

Temi's parents and my parents are quite similar, they want the same things for us – a good job, a good husband, three to four grandchildren, Christmases spent in Nigeria, etc. But the circumstances are different. While Temi's parents guided her in the direction of the life they clearly wanted for her, Temi, as the youngest of three, knew she had an opportunity to do life on her own terms, with fewer consequences to be fearful of, because she had two older brothers who had already ticked all the necessary achievement boxes: career in law/finance/medicine/engineering; marriage. I, on the other hand, am the youngest of three girls.

Sons in Nigerian families are like crowning glories: they continue the family legacy, keep the name going, take up the mantle when the father dies. But in a house with three daughters, my parents found no room for error and sought to mould us into perfect women: impeccable candidates for the perfect wives for the perfect sons-in-law. Our entire lives were mapped out in Excel spreadsheets where they calculated various probabilities and formulated a strategy for each one of us. My oldest sister was to become a doctor, as eldest siblings should; my middle sister was to become a lawyer; and I, an engineer. I played my role well, was largely obedient, didn't talk back, took some severe childhood reproachments in my stride, resolved to forgive them and move on the next day. In spite of my best efforts to stick to the plan, my parents were never satisfied, and found reasons to pick at my behaviour, from the way I had incorrectly greeted one of my elders, to how I should have also skipped a year like Temi but hadn't worked hard enough. Where my sisters were silent and even smiling at every reprimand, my mother said my eyes were vacant and my mind elsewhere. Where my sisters beamed at the chance to get an uncle they'd never met another plate of rice and stew with two extra pieces of meat – regardless of what the caterer says – I looked ungrateful for the opportunity to show respect to my elders. My father – in one of the few times he spoke during my mother's many lectures and admonishments – said that I behaved as though obedience was below me. I didn't fit, I understood later, and so they worked me harder, chastened me more often. My success was going to have to come at a higher price, they decided.

Even now, although I am married and technically – we do not have a prenuptial agreement – richer than both my well-off doctor and lawyer sisters put together, my parents, particularly my mother, still regularly discover ways in which I am inadequate. Temi knows this, has observed my parents' constant dissatisfaction with me ever since we became friends, and so she believes my marriage hasn't solved anything. That I have simply swapped one prison – living at home with my parents – for another. But she's wrong.

My husband calls again halfway through this thought, and I let my phone ring through to voicemail even though I'm looking at his face illuminating my phone. It's a picture of us on our honeymoon in Italy, one of those photos taken by the man rowing our gondola. It's blurry but it's one of the only photos of the two of us that I like, so it's been my photo for his contact ever since. He calls again and this time I count three vibrations before I pick up. Temi even looks over on the second ring and I wag my finger at her, take a sip of wine that I forgot no longer exists in my glass, and then answer. This time I don't put him on speaker.

I'm not feeling well, he says. I don't ask him why, because I know him well enough to know that he's about to tell me why regardless of whether or not I ask. I hear him sigh into the phone, and I'm sure his left arm is currently draped over his head, which is the pose he normally assumes when he's feeling unwell. Today has been . . . I just want a quiet night in. I had to sort out so much stuff that doesn't have anything to do with my work and it's killed me. I'm exhausted. I feel like I've been hit by a bus. He goes on for a while. He has a thing about using exaggerative phrasing. He is prone to it when he feels vulnerable. Then he says: Is she definitely staying for dinner? I look towards Temi, who is now standing by the wine cooler and holding a bottle of wine up to her face like she's trying to read the list of ingredients, even though there isn't one. Yes, I say slowly. What about the guy she's seeing? Doesn't he want to see her? Which one? I say, and he sighs again. He reminds me once more that he's so, so tired and wants to leave work early, and that he doesn't want Japanese food any more. Okay, so what do you want? I ask. Peace, he says, and I can tell his hand is over his mouth because the sound is muffled. And quiet, he says, having lifted his hand. An evening spent with my wife. I'll work on it, I say, and then hang up.

Temi brings over the bottle that she's been squinting at, says that she wants to try a red. We've been drinking a bottle of white since she arrived and usually red ends in disaster, which is fine, but I'd prefer not to bear the brunt of it today. That red is one my husband is saving to drink on a special occasion because he says it's difficult to get. So I make a face at the bottle and suggest a rosé that I bought from Oddbins a while ago and never opened because I forgot about it until now. She's not pleased about the idea, says the thought of me setting foot inside an Oddbins shop sounds very pedestrian, but she goes along with it, and I pour her half of a half-glass. If she notices she doesn't say anything, just takes a small sip and then asks what we're doing next. I shrug and pour myself a full glass, consider the mechanics of manufacturing a 'quiet night in', per my husband's request.

*

I never really bothered with boys at school. The only time we encountered them was at our school dances where the chaperones would watch us like hawks, and only the girls that people called skanks would go behind the building afterwards and kiss the boys while leaning against the swimming-pool fence. I also noticed that a lot of the girls would regularly swap boyfriends. Cathy's Year 9 boyfriend would later become her close friend Delilah's Year 10 boyfriend. It was a unique kind of incest.

I was sceptical about anyone who expressed interest in me, mostly because Temi always reminded me that none of them were good enough for me, and also because they weren't. (The boys who were interested in me were all short. I mean my height, about five foot six, or shorter. Maybe I'm old-fashioned or superficial, but I had aspirations of looking up into my husband's eyes, not down.) There was Aiden, an Irish boy who knew how to pronounce my name properly and believed this made him some kind of rare and very spectacular person. I explained to him that Temi, my mother, father, siblings and all my extended family possessed the same ability, and rejected his offer to go to Blockbuster together and steal a film. There was Ash, one of three mixed-race boys in our year group, who all the white girls were in love with. We didn't have a word for him back then, but now we know the term is 'hotep'. I went on one date with him, which wasn't really a date because we were just revising in his living room where his older sister was also doing her homework, but afterwards he referred to me as his Black Queen and changed his name in my phone to Black King. I would have stayed with him for the status, because while I was with him the white girls became incredibly nice to me, but his mother got a job somewhere in the countryside, a place that isn't Cornwall but might as well be, so he left school and only texted me once three months later to ask for nudes.

Then there was Gbenga. During his tenure, Temi and I did not talk about boys. She'll never admit that she was in love with him, but I knew she was because of the way she acted around him. She would nod if he said something in class that she thought contained intelligence, or she would point out if his shoelaces were on the verge of coming undone just so she would have something to say to him, or we would eat lunch with him and his friends and she would stay silent while he was talking – wouldn't interrupt or make a cutting comment, she would just sit and listen. And for Temi, who has opinions about what you ordered at her birthday dinner in 2011, that was a big deal. It meant that there was something special about him. I will admit that Gbenga was good-looking for whatever now-questionable standards we had as sixteen-year-olds, and he was as interesting as teenage boys can be, but for him to be the object of my friend's affection – or whatever her version of affection is – was a significant and peculiar departure from the most unromantic person I've ever met.

For as long as we'd been friends, Temi had said that men were not part of her plan. They were too weak to survive the inevitable apocalypse so there was no reason to engage with them in any substantive way, she said when I asked her to explain what she meant. She had never considered men to be equal to women, so I'd always assumed that she had no serious interest in them, and never would. She cited her brothers and father as prime examples as to why I would never catch her pining over one. Men were like those pans that say non-stick and then you fry one egg and the whole pan is ruined, she said once. So when Gbenga and I became friends while waiting for our parents to pick us up from after-school activities, and when he kissed me behind the girls' school PE shed, I never told her. I thought she'd be disappointed in me for being linked to a boy in that way, and our friendship was more important than a teenage boy. She never would have admitted how she felt about him, but I couldn't imagine a conversation in which I told her and it didn't sound like I was confessing a sin. I played it out in my head: I would explain the time we spent together, the circumstances for the kiss, double down on how mediocre it was while she looked at me, arms crossed. She would laugh at me, probably, and then reel off a list of his negative traits. Reminding me that even if I did like him, as she always said, men were not our equals.

Regardless, after the kiss Gbenga and I never really spoke again. He was dating racially ambiguous Cara in Year 10 two weeks later, and I was back to remembering that Temi was right.

My sister once said she thought my friendship with Temi was unhealthy. She wasn't the first person to say it, but I found it funny regardless. She said that Temi controlled me. Like, she has this weird hold over you. I would say that to an extent she did, like any friends have a hold on each other, like two people in any kind of relationship do. There is a known reliance, a shared understanding that without one, there cannot be the other in its fullest form. That hold was the very reason we became friends in the first place; it was our special bond, the thing that kept us together when girls in our school were falling out over shared boyfriends, when school friends lost touch after they went to different universities, or when one friend got married and the unmarried friend suddenly became invisible.

The thing about Temi is that she knows me. She understands the way my mind works – she watched me interact with my parents for years – she knows how I am likely to react in certain situations, whether or not I will like a person within a few seconds of meeting them, knows how to convince me of something, and knows when I can't be convinced. She knew that I was desperate to escape the clutches of my parents by going to a university in London and leaving home but that I was too scared to say it out loud, so she intervened, lobbied my parents and convinced them on the academic grounds they so deeply respected.

Similarly, I know her. I know when she is upset or angry but doesn't want to say that she is, when she is stressed but instead pretends that she is completely unbothered. I know Temi had opinions about whether my marriage would alter our friendship in an unchangeably negative way. But the opposite happened. My friendship with Temi became stronger after I got married. Once I was no longer working and only had to answer to my parents quarterly, I found that I had so much more time and money to spend with and on her (she always orders the most expensive thing on the menu when she knows I'm paying using the card from the joint account I have with my husband, to which I contribute a grand total of nothing). I had new and unexpected stories to share with her, unfamiliar oddities from the uncharted waters of marriage we could laugh about or interrogate. That included what intimacy was like now that I was married, what waking up to the same person every day was like, what deciding on what to buy for the week was like, what passive-aggressive arguing after three glasses of expensive wine was like, what walking around Ikea for six hours was like without even stopping by the restaurant to eat meatballs because we have food at home.

The day before my traditional, my mother took one of my hands and lightly shook it by the wrist as she gave me some advice that I can't say I've taken. Keep your husband happy with you, she said, then tilted her chin down into her chest and looked over imaginary glasses at me. Mm? Mind your own. If you have any problems, keep them between yourself – she poked me in the chest – and your husband. Don't just open your mouth and scatter your marital business to anyone. But Temi isn't just anyone. When I told her about how he always yawns exactly three times before he falls asleep, she threw her head back and laughed. When I told her about how he insists on holding my hand when we cross roads together, she pretended to put her finger down her throat to make herself gag. Temi loves these stories, sharing in a kind of forbidden intimacy to which only she, myself and my husband are privy. An intimacy that she should not be a part of, but one that, if anything, makes us closer.

*

I tell Temi to think about what we should do while I use the toilet. I take my daily vitamins out of the bathroom cupboard, pop one in my mouth and follow it with a handful of filtered water from the tap. A ritual performed out of responsibility rather than desire. As I walk back into the kitchen I hear her laughing, tapping one of her rings against the table and throwing her head back. Is that what I said? Really? She shouts as though whoever she's conversing with is half a mile away and not, in fact, on the phone – my phone – as I discover when I return to the table and find her FaceTiming our mutual sister-in-law.

Three months after I married my husband, Temi's brother became engaged to my husband's sister. They'd met at our wedding, and soon after, when they realised that they could tolerate being alone together for more than a few hours without arguing, they took into account their being older than us (they're both in their mid-thirties) and decided to get married sooner rather than later. At their wedding both Temi and I were bridesmaids, and in her speech – my sister-in-law made a point of giving one despite it being unconventional, which Temi said I should have done at mine – spoke about what a joy it was to have a sister-in-law who felt more like a friend. I remembered again how she and Temi spent a significant portion of my wedding together, and knew she wasn't talking about me. I watched as Temi smiled back at her and downed the rest of her Hennessy.

I go to the counter and pour myself some more wine and pull out a half-empty packet of nuts that I remembered are in the cupboard by the sink. When I sit down at the table, Temi makes a face at me like she feels betrayed. Where did you get those from? she says, and I gesture towards the cupboard. So when I was opening all the cupboards like a hungry animal you were just laughing at me knowing there were nuts hidden away? Give me, she says, pulling the packet towards herself. She rests the phone against the vase on the table so we can both be seen. Hi hi! my sister-in-law says, waving from what looks like the pool in her Victoria Island home's back garden. I wave and smile, point at my mouth to signal that there's food in it so I can't talk. She says, Oh don't worry, and then remarks on how jealous she is that we're drinking. Why aren't you drinking? Temi says, shoving a handful of the honey-roasted cashews in her mouth. I note how big a handful it is and eye the rest of the bag to make sure I get an equal share. Well, my sister-in-law says, looking from side to side as though anyone is listening to her conversation when she is clearly alone, it's actually why I called. Temi looks at me and I shrug, pulling the packet of nuts towards myself as she looks back at the phone. A text message from my husband arrives and appears as notification on the top of the screen. As Temi swipes up to dismiss it, below it my sister-in-law is making a baby-bump gesture. Temi drops her head to the table, bangs her fist three times. All you people and your procreating, she moans. My sister-in-law is laughing. First this one – Temi points at me with her lips – and now you. I won't babysit, you know, I won't take responsibility for another contribution to the destruction of this planet. She reaches for the nuts but finds they're not where she left them and gives me a look as she stretches for the almost-empty packet. My sister-in-law stops laughing suddenly and looks directly at the camera, brings it close to her face. Wait, what do you mean first this one? SIS! she shouts, her excessive volume distorting the sound from my phone. Are you and my baby brother pregnant? I chew the tiny piece of nut left in my mouth for as long as I can. Temi answers for me, tilts the camera to herself to say NO then places it back the way it was, both of us in view.

Congratulations, I say, my smile barely reaching my cheeks. Then, How far along are you? She points the camera towards her stomach and I can tell that she is pushing out. I'm three months, but I'm barely showing. Like what's the point in being pregnant if you're not even showing? No one is opening doors for me or forbidding me from using sharp objects like nail scissors yet. Apparently the fanfare only comes when you look like you ate your twin in the womb and didn't fully digest her. Anyway, what does Temi mean first this one? Oh, I say, we're just working on it. What? He didn't say! She says it like she and my husband are super-close even though I've seen him turn his phone over when he sees that she's calling him. Anyway, enjoy the working on it, you know? She winks as she picks up the juice next to her and sips through a straw. But you're okay to drink even though you're trying? Temi takes a generous swig of her wine and swirls it in her mouth as she turns to stare at me. I think it's fine, I say, and press my finger on to the surface of the table to pick up any leftover crumbs that might have honey fla-vouring on them. Does my brother think it's okay? He thinks a lot of things, I say, and my sister-in-law laughs, covering her mouth. You see, Temi, this could be you, she says. Temi scoffs and says H A as loud as she can: My mind is above this temporal plane of procreation, being married and withhold-ing good things from myself like alcohol – she lifts her glass as if toasting someone, probably herself – that you people are on. I have bigger things to concern myself with. Plus, I'm not even convinced that our sister here wants kids. Didn't you have to be convinced? she says, looking at me. Didn't it take a dramatic/tense/threatening conversation with your mother-in-law or something? Oh my lord my mother, my sister-in-law says, she was on me about her grandson lit-erally the day we came back from our honeymoon. Yeah, she wasn't pleased when I said I wanted to wait a while, I say. I think she's going to be waiting forever, Temi says, and downs the rest of the wine in her glass, then goes to get the bottle to top herself up.

So you don't want kids? my sister-in-law asks me, sitting up a little on her sunlounger, her large-brimmed hat obscuring half of one eye. She says she does, Temi says as she walks back to the table, unscrewing the bottle of rosé that I left on the kitchen counter behind us. But, she continues, I've seen her try harder to find a Korean restaurant that makes their bulgogi just the way she likes it than she is trying to get pregnant. I push my empty wine glass towards her and she pours me a generous amount, finishing off the bottle, in view of the camera. Temi sees my sister-in-law squinting and turns the bottle around to look at the label. It's only like seven per cent, she says, it won't kill your little niece or nephew, don't worry. My sister-in-law laughs and sips her juice again. But you're off birth control? I nod. Temi looks over at me, tilts her head slightly to one side. How are you finding the period pains? my sister-in-law says. They're nasty, right? With birth control it was like two people were stabbing me from the inside every month; now it feels like twelve. Yeah, I know what you mean, I say, and Temi raises her eyebrows and smirks at me.

On the phone my sister-in-law raises her voice slightly at someone out of the frame as she hands them her half-empty glass of juice: Jollof *and* fried rice please . . . and maybe some egusi if we have any left over from yesterday? The baby likes variety. She places her hands in her lap like a children's TV presenter about to sign off – Okay, my lovely sisters, I have to go. The husband will be home soon and I expect he'll want to be checking on the baby, you know? That is disgusting, Temi says, and my sister-in-law begins to stand up and then sits back down suddenly. Oh. Don't tell my brother. I called him first but he didn't pick up so I'll try him again now. I want to tell him myself that he's going to be an uncle. Neither Temi nor I respond, and she pauses, as though waiting for a reaction, then winks and reaches over to end the call without saying goodbye. Tell me the truth, Temi says, putting my phone face down. You haven't had period pains in about five years. I lick the remaining sugar from the cashews off my fingers. Do I call you every time I stub my toe? she scoffs as she crumples the empty packet of nuts. You know unless there's at least half a pint of blood I'm not interested in your medical concerns. Well, I'm not taking the pill any more, I say. She shrugs, unconvinced. Why do you even want a baby? Why not. It's not like I'll have to take care of it anyway. His mother will move in, even though I have explicitly requested that she doesn't, and she'll do everything for me. Temi sucks in her cheeks for a second. And when it's sixteen and has been spending time with Cressida and Maxwell from next door who regularly tell their mother to eff off when she doesn't order oysters for dinner and it comes home and tries that with you? she says. I laugh as I drink from my glass, make a pleasantly surprised face because I wasn't expecting to have taken so much in one gulp – Temi, come on, what are boarding schools for? She covers her mouth as if someone has told a dirty joke, then tips her head approvingly in my direction. Your poor husband.

*

The first time my husband and Temi met was the same day I met him – at a family function. Temi came to all our family events and my husband came with his parents and sister. They were neighbours of our aunt and uncle who were hosting. My husband stood in a corner with his sister judging everyone, and Temi picked them out as snobs and made a point of going over to talk to them. Of course, as with most things she suggests, she said I had to go with her. We agreed that he was attractive for someone of his sex even if he was clearly a snob, and as we made eye contact with the two of them, Temi said that he was staring at me. I think perhaps he was just looking at the two women who were whispering to each other as they made a direct approach towards him.

We were nineteen and home from university the summer after our first year – Temi took a very risky gap year (something that Nigerian children do not do; parents respond with: What is gap year? Are you between the train and the platform?) – and he was in the first year of his masters. I was impressed when his sister revealed that piece of information, and Temi elbowed me in the ribs, later said men rewarding other men at institutions that were in the first instance created only for men was not impressive. He didn't say a lot – his sister revealed that he had been dragged there by their parents – but up close appeared to have a good face, nice teeth, and no sweat patches or food on his white T-shirt, despite it being a hot day and a barbecue. His sister was much more our speed. She was funny, explained that they were in fact judging people, and invited us to confirm her suspicions about my family members, most of which were true. I noticed when my husband laughed or smiled at them. His sister is a lot more like Temi than I am: she is very firm in her opinions, likes to insult or make fun of my husband whenever she can, and for the most part couldn't care less about her parents' expectations of her, though she has achieved them all: doctor, married into a wealthy family to expand her existing wealth and influential social networks, doesn't have an Instagram or Twitter account, only a mostly idle Facebook account where she occasionally shares links to posts about medical findings or seasonal messages from Sheryl Sandberg or Michelle Obama as though she is reposting a friend of hers. After my husband and I got engaged, Temi would sometimes send me pictures of herself and my husband's sister at lunch or dinner or shopping, or at a private exhibition somewhere with an SW1, W1 or SW3 postcode. She says at least once a month that between my husband and his sister, I have chosen the inferior of the two siblings to associate with.

Temi and my husband, though, have always had something odd between them. I didn't think that she would necessarily welcome him with open arms but I didn't anticipate her reaction. She had strongly advocated for me to put myself out there at university but when I told her I was going on a date with him a few weeks after the barbecue, her eyes flared open. I don't know, she said. We were in her childhood bedroom and I was sitting on the floor while she lay on her bed flipping through a textbook and pretending to have a photographic memory instead of helping me take out my braids like she had promised to. She'd never had a serious boyfriend, at least not to my knowledge, but she seemed set against the idea. So I cancelled the date. Then I thought about why I'd cancelled it and realised that the reason was Temi's and not my own, and I was supposed to be making my own decisions per Temi's instructions, so I went on the date. When I told Temi it had gone well, she winced. As I continued to see him, I thought their mutual animosity might peacefully cancel itself out: she unhappy with his entire existence; he displeased with her frequent presence in mine. As I imagined it, whenever they would walk into a room where the other was they would exchange tight smiles and say 'You good Yeah you Yeah good' and they would agree that was the extent of their conversations. I wasn't naive enough to picture them as best friends because I know that the way I interact with each of them is different. I like that time with Temi is fun and selfish and carefree, and afterwards I can return home to my husband who is calm and unchallenging. That being said, I didn't expect them to be sworn enemies. That my husband would loudly exhale whenever he hears Temi's voice on the phone in the background, or sees her shoes in the hallway when he comes home. The new and creative ways Temi would find to insult my husband right in front of me, or bring up memories of our friendship from before I knew him, just to remind him that she's been in my life longer than he has. I started to really notice it right after I got engaged, and then it got worse during the wedding planning, when they argued, a lot: about the song my husband and I would have our first dance to, about the cake tasting that she came to, about what she thought my husband should say in his vows to me.

It is strange, and every so often uncomfortable, when the insults become more pointed and personal. But it's also entertaining. I like to say almost nothing, see where it goes. It's fun to watch them get increasingly incensed by the presence of the other, by the small snide comments here and there, by the competition to see who will leave a room first. Only rarely has it become a real fight, where one of them says or does something that tips the other over the edge, and it goes from being funny to a little distressing and awkward. Usually those moments occur when an exorbitant amount of alcohol has been consumed.

But I can't take sides between the two most important people in my life – I can't tell Temi to stop – so I make like Ronan Keating and say nothing at all. I decided after the first uncomfortable interaction that they were both adults and I could neither control them nor reprimand them. I simply observe.

Tonight, this is how I think it will go: my husband will come home, tired, lethargic, working hard to be unbothered by Temi's reappearance in our home after a month of respite, and doing all that he can to ignore her. Temi, meanwhile, will watch him being sluggish and saying very little, and find ways to provoke him. Like when she made fun of his beard and how he could only grow it about two centimetres from his face, or when she said his feet – size ten – were small for a man his size. He's six foot two. He will try to take the insults in his stride, like he always does, which is how I'll know that he'll be even more annoyed later. And then, once we've had a few more glasses of wine, and Temi's not-so-underhanded comments have evolved and I have hidden my face in my glass to laugh at them, maybe, just maybe, a shouting match will begin.

*

When Temi returned from her gap year at the end of the summer before we started university, she unveiled her master plan. She'd been abroad 'interning' with her lawyer aunt in America and had finally worked out how she would spend the rest of her life. BMFM, she said, like I was supposed to know what it meant. She tilted her head towards me as she unpacked her suitcases, various new clothes still with their tags on folded carefully inside.

By Myself, For Myself, she said. My own decisions, made purely for myself, with consideration only for the environment and the NHS, she said, tapping the side of her forehead with her nail. I questioned the 'by myself' part first. She rolled her eyes, annoyed that she had to explain it to me, and tossed me a folded postcard with the Golden Gate Bridge on it. Apparently people still send postcards to their friends when they're on holiday, she said, but the queues at the post office were going to make us late for our Nobu reservation so you're getting this now. She sat down at the edge of her bed and looked at me. I understand your whole wanting boys/ men/males thing, I do, but husbands want wives and wives are a different species to single women. Single women are concerned only with themselves and get to eat dinner and put on weight and lose it whenever they want. Having a long-term boyfriend or a husband is like having another set of parents. Ew. No, not like that, obviously, but it's just one more person who wants a piece of you. A piece of your time, a piece of your money, a piece of your body when eventually they are ready to breed and stick you with the children all day. She patted my hand. One day, it will make sense.

I watched her unpack the rest of her things, observing the way she winced at and discarded the clothes she'd taken with her but took care with the new ones, smoothing them down before finding a place for them in her wardrobe. I was quiet for a while and she noticed. Look, you're your own person. BMFM, it might not be for you. But I think you're better than anyone in your life gives you credit for and you could – if you wanted to – actually be happy living for yourself for once. She sat down on the bed again and looked at me as I fiddled with a bent edge of the postcard. No more trying to make yourself look like a carbon copy of your sisters, no more letting people talk down to you or tell you what not to say, what to wear, how to behave, which career path to follow. Every decision, up to you. I considered her idea, thought about the endless conversations I'd had with my parents that summer, and agreed. BMFM, I said, opening the postcard out. The message on it had clearly been written in haste: *Sorry your parents are boring! Temi xx.*

*

I might nap, she says, yawning. We're in the living room sat on our designated corner sofas, raising our voices slightly to be heard across the room from each other. I think that rosé is going to put me to sleep, she says, fluffing one of the cushions to use as a pillow. I know that she probably will sleep, but that when she wakes up I'll be expected to have something fun planned. It's almost two p.m. on my watch and I should probably replace the Snickers bars from earlier, so I tell her she can sleep in the guest room while I go out. I think about taking the bottle of red my husband's been saving with me because I know that she'll wait until she's heard the car leave the drive before she goes to look for it, so I carry it upstairs, her eyes following the bottle through the open living-room door, and hide it in my husband's side of the walk-in wardrobe.

Before I leave I drink half a small bottle of Evian, and in the car find a packet of gum in the drinks holder and put two pieces in my mouth. I am sober enough to walk in a straight line and my vision isn't blurred, and I remember to check all the mirrors so I decide I'm safe enough to drive too. My phone vibrates on the passenger seat and I find a text from my husband – *I too would like to be a man of leisure* – and interpret it for what it is, a cry for help, and decide to drop him off a late lunch. I didn't exactly warn him that Temi was back from her trip or that she would be coming over today. He always mentions how his colleagues' significant others bring lunch for them or randomly 'pop in' to visit so I have inferred that this is something he appreciates me doing. And after this morning

I know that a display of affection will go a ways to fixing whatever problem my still not being pregnant has begun to expose. I check my breath and then my face in the rear-view mirror. My very thin eyeliner hasn't smudged, though my lip tint has significantly faded, so I use the hand cream we keep in the glove compartment – hands that look like the Sahara Desert are not hands that should be seen in public – and a tissue to wipe it off completely. I make a last double-check of my breath – if my husband smells the wine he'll be annoyed. He probably knows I've been drinking anyway, because that's what Temi and I always do when we're together – he once slipped a leaflet for A A into Temi's bag when she came over and she actually cried laughing when she found it some time later, texted me to tell him well done – but he doesn't believe in accusations without evidence, so he won't say anything unless he can prove it. I reverse confidently out of the drive, confident that I am able to do it, only to forget to release the gate and nearly collide with it.

On either side of us live other married couples of similar ages with similar dynamics, though the couple to the left of us – Priya and Mark – both work. We do dinners with them every now and again, and spend two to three hours passive-aggressively trying to show one another up. I had some initial reservations (none of which I voiced) about living in a house with a gated driveway, within a gated community, but I can never remember what they were.

Outside our gated community are various overpriced independent grocery shops that sell bulbs of garlic at two pounds each, or, during their summer sale, one large onion for one pound fifty. There's a butcher whose shop is laid out like a design studio, with his sister's equally non-functional fishmonger next door. A few doors down from the 'locally sourced' bakery there's a florist that assures you – via a hand-painted sign on its storefront window – that the flowers have been picked gently and with love, so that you can pass the love on. Meanwhile, inside, chopping the stems aggressively in front of you and saying, That'll be sixty-four eighty please. But we like it here. Temi asked me once if I thought we fit, and I wasn't exactly sure what she meant. We were only the third Black couple to move into the gated community in its entire eight-year existence, but we knew that the moment we showed the residency board my husband's last two pay cheques our 'fitting in' wouldn't be a problem. Money makes everyone fit when it needs to.

Before exiting the neighbourhood entirely I stop at the bakery I went to earlier this morning and the woman at the counter says, Oh twice in one day, you must really be hungry, and I resist the urge to explain that humans generally eat three meals a day and so a second visit really isn't that unprecedented. When I get back to the car I have a missed call and two texts from Temi: *Your guest-room pillows are embarrassing. Going to pick up some more snacks and wine – think I still have my spare key.* Then the next message: *Your wine selection is also embarrassing.*

The parking attendant at my husband's office has got to know me from my visits once every few months, so she waves me through happily, deftly passing a permit to me as I drive through. I make a point to smile in response to her 'Hello', just in case the minty smell of the gum has waned on the drive over. Inside, the receptionist on the main floor smiles awkwardly as she points me towards the lifts as though I'm a stranger, even though we once had a ten-minute conversation about the products I use in my hair to keep it moisturised, and I took her number and sent her links to the natural hair bloggers I follow. I smile back and go past her to the lifts I already know the location of, and press the button when I'm inside. The doors are just closing as one of my husband's colleagues, a man we have nicknamed Overshare, sticks a hand between the doors, somehow quietly shouts 'Sorry!' and then makes a mock-surprised face when he sees that it's me in the lift. I know how much he loves small talk, so I mentally prepare three basic questions and reciprocal answers that should see us to the fourteenth floor. Oh my goodness! He opens his arms as if he's going to receive a hug but I shake my head and he drops them, moves next to me and faces the doors instead. Gosh I haven't seen you in ages. How are things? I was just telling your husband that we need to have you two round for dinner. We keep missing you with work commitments and illnesses and all that mess and we need to nail down a date! He keeps boasting about your wine collection and I fancy a bottle to test that theory! I smile, because I know I'm not supposed to respond, only give him a chance to catch his breath before he continues. My wife was just saying that she wants to show you what she's wearing to the next party, so she can get your approval! You know, I was literally just saying to your husband last week – or no, was it the week before, because we were getting salads and it was a bit warmer out so I wasn't wearing a jacket but then it started to rain and he didn't have his umbrella – but then it rained a bit last week too – no it was last week – I think it was last week anyway. But yeah, I was telling him that I'd really missed out on the party year before last. Obviously, that was before we got the new bo—The doors to the lift open on the tenth floor where people bustle in and it's no longer just the two of us, people have occupied the space between us and it would now be rude for him to talk over them, but he only pauses, then continues to talk over the people between us: Before we got the new boss. He's had two wives since we started and it's only been just over a year. Got kids with both of them, too. Apparently he was working on kids with the latest while he was still married to the last. Meanwhile some of us can only handle one woman at a time! The woman next to him turns and I imagine an expression on her face that communicates disdain and he looks from me down to her and says, No one is forcing you to listen to me, then looks back up at me over her head, continues. Speaking of kids, are you expecting? Looking a bit more spherical than the last time I saw yo—At that two of the other women in the lift turn to him and one of them says, Are you being serious? as the lift doors open on to the fourteenth floor. Everyone files out. I make sure I move to leave the lift before the woman next to me does, and by the time Overshare has noticed, I'm already walking through the glass doors and finding my way to my husband's office.

As I open the door, my husband looks up.

Two

I speak first when my wife walks into my office. Between the two of us she always likes to wait until I've said something so she knows how the conversation will go, how to react. I say, Oh, thank God, and force a smile while she looks me over, spies the spot of green juice on my shirt. She scrunches up her face, as if the smell of the juice is overwhelmingly pungent. I explain that I spilled it earlier that morning as she closes the door, walks over and pulls out my chair to sit on my lap. I bury my face in her chest and she rubs the back of my head, something she only ever does on rare occasions when I've had a bad day and look pathetic. We stay like that for a few seconds, until I remember that if my wife is here—Did you . . . leave her at home? I ask. She lifts her head from the top of mine and stands up, walks over to my window where the city sits below. Yeah, but she's sleeping, or she was. What does that even mean? She said she was going to nap but then she also said she was going to get some more wine. She brings a finger to her forehead as she realises that she didn't mean to expose that she'd been drinking but she and her friend always drink when they're together so it's not a surprise. It's not even three p.m., I say, how much could she possibly have had to drink? My wife doesn't turn around, but shrugs, says her friend came over at twelve and they started drinking a little after that. She drops her shoulders and sighs when she sees the twisted mouth on my face. Oh my goodness, it's not the alcohol that's the problem, is it? It won't make a difference. It's fine. Calm down. She wanders over to the bookshelf where she told me to put a number of thick architecture-related books, a dictionary and a couple of fiction titles. It will make you look like you're interested in more than one thing, but not in a way that makes it clear that that's what you want people to think, that's why I suggested only a couple of fiction books, she'd said. She picks one of the smaller architecture books off the shelf and starts flicking through it. Stop staring at me, she says. As we both know, I'm not pregnant, and even if I was, a few glasses wouldn't do anything. I cross my arms and watch her exhale dramatically. Might not do anything, I say, but driving under the influence could kill you.

*

The baby conversation started barely a month after we got married, when my parents, as Nigerians do, asked when the grandchildren would be arriving. My wife explained that she wanted to just be married for a while, to which my mother said, You will 'just be married' your entire life, what kind of excuse is that? But eventually, the questions stopped.

Now that we've been married for three years, the questions have started up again. I tried to prepare my wife for the most recent conversation with my mother that I knew would be coming by bringing up the subject at dinner in a way that I hoped seemed nonchalant. While I picked at some pieces of plantain, I mentioned that one of my co-workers, who had been married for a year less than us, was expecting her first child. My wife didn't bite, so I elaborated, explaining that they'd been trying for a few months and were really excited to be starting a family. That's nice, she finally said, putting a half-forkful of fried rice in her mouth. I tried then to make the unborn child seem more appealing: She said it's brought them so much closer together – the baby, I mean. My wife nodded and passed a quick smile across the table. I opened my mouth to speak again, to buttress the point, and I think a small sound even came out, but she lifted her hand, with the fork still in it, and I stopped. Why don't you, instead of walking the length of the River Nile around the point, just say what it is you want to say? I put my cutlery down and interlaced my fingers over my plate, tucked my crossed ankles underneath the chair. I've been thinking that maybe we could talk about having children again – or at least a child, singular. Right, she said and then nothing else, so I felt the need to fill the silence. We've been married for a while now, and you know, we both agreed that we wanted to have kids—I did not, she interrupted, but continue. Internally I struggled not to remind her that she had, in fact, told my mother that we would start trying in 'a while', which didn't mean never, but I overcame the urge to prove my correctness and her incorrectness, and tried to focus on the task of convincing her. We're financially stable – well, more than stable; I'm at a place in my career where I make my own hours; we've done, at least for now, all the travelling that I feel like we want to do; and we're happy, or something similar, I would like to think. And more importantly, we'd make great parents – you'd be a great mother. She didn't say anything for at least fifteen to twenty seconds, at which point I regretted the full-fat cliché about her being a good mother, and also applauded myself for not having said *make* a good mother, a comment she would never have forgiven me for.

Eventually, she sipped her drink – Hennessy on ice, like a true Nigerian – and said, One child, and on one condition. I smiled to try and lighten the mood. It's not a business deal, we don't need conditions. She repeated herself: One condition. I can't agree to it until you've said it, I said. I'm about to say it, she said. Then I'll wait. I leaned back in my chair and crossed my arms. Your mother is under no circumstances allowed to move in at any point ever – even if she is on the brink of death and reaching painfully over to the other side – to look after the child. That is non-negotiable. It seemed simple enough a condition, so I agreed to it.

So we've been trying. Checking ovulation and adding vitamins to our diets that are scientifically proven to increase the chances of conceiving, taking two pregnancy tests a month and readjusting our expectations every time. Most things have come easily to me, and I expected children to be the same, but our doctor tells us that it takes most people six months to a year of trying before anything happens. Patience doesn't come easily to me, so I am trying to cultivate it. I'm unsure whether my patience is supposed to reward me with what I want sooner or later, though. The rules on it are unclear and results vary.

*

You're so dramatic, my wife says, and puts the book back on the shelf. I had maybe one and a half glasses and I ate as well. I drove here just fine. Anyway, I came to say hello, not to talk extensively about ethanol-infused liquids. How's your day going? Apart from the juice. I grimace and lean my elbows on the desk. I – am trying to stay positive, despite the circumstances, I say. She nods and walks to the other side of my desk, and I can tell she wants to ask me something so I motion for her to sit down on the chair just behind her. She considers it, and opts to lean against the armrest instead. Why don't you come home now, work the rest of the day from home? The last time she suggested that she did not really have any plans for me to 'work' from home. I smile and wonder if she's suggesting the same thing again, and she says, No, Temi is coming back later, remember? My smile disappears and I shake my head. I barely find it possible to exist when she is in our house, how am I supposed to concentrate while she's there? My wife smiles sympathetically. We'll be downstairs, she says in a quiet voice, like I'm a child who doesn't know how houses and sound work. And you'll talk to her? I ask. She sighs and looks away as she responds, And I'll talk to her. And explain that, as agreed, unannounced weekday visits are also unwelcome visits? Sure. I squint at her – I am unconvinced. Stop doing that, she says, watching my forehead crease. When the wind changes—My face will stay like that – I know, I say, finishing her sentence for her. Look, just think about it, she says. Clearly your day isn't getting any better by staying here, and if you do stay, your boss will probably ask you to do some more of someone else's work too. Better to go home and be miserable within reach of some alcohol rather than half a bottle of six-pound green juice, no?

*

Meeting my wife is something my sister will always take credit for. On a weekend I was back home, taking a break from my masters classes at uni, my parents dragged us to the next-door neighbours' barbecue. My sister had opened the window to look at what was happening in their back garden, which is to say a lot of noise, a lot of smoke coming from the barbecue and a large number of people packed into a space barely sufficient to fit them. She said it looked fun. It's not the word I would have used.

It was chaotic, the two people who were supposed to be manning the barbecue were having an animated conversation a full metre away from it; I could see mostly empty black bags tacked on to the sides of garden chairs while squashed cans of Coke, Pepsi and Sprite were scattered all over the garden. The music was so loud we all had to shout as my mother introduced us to the host, who was holding a paper plate full of jollof rice, two chicken bones, some moin moin and what looked like a half-scoop of one of those Nigerian salads that includes boiled eggs, sweetcorn and grated carrots. Our parents went off in search of food, and my sister and I – we are picky eaters – opted for cans of ginger beer swimming in the large blue bucket of what was once ice, and found a corner in the garden where we were furthest away from the barbecue and the speakers. We stood and judged everyone around us – their questionable sartorial choices, the way they were chewing their food (mouth open) – pausing occasionally to complain about how few people our age had decided to attend. I was asking my sister if she wanted another ginger beer when she interrupted me to subtly indicate, using as little mouth movement as possible, that two women were walking directly towards us.

This is where the stories differ. My wife says her best friend encouraged her to go for me because she could tell I liked her; my wife's best friend says the exact same thing, embellishing it with details like I bit my lip or licked them; and my sister will tell you a version of the truth which is closer to, but still not, it. What really happened is that as the two of them walked over to us my sister elbowed me in the ribs, and even though I knew what the elbow in the ribs meant, I didn't know to whom she was referring, and more than that, her elbow in the ribs was actually painful and so I coughed, a cough I now know both my wife and her best friend interpreted as my nervousness at my wife walking up to me. I *was* nervous, but less because of how beautiful my wife was, and more because I was looking at my wife's best friend, whose facial expression was somewhere between deviousness and smugness, neither of which I could see reason for. So, they walked up to us, my wife staying quiet, like me, while her best friend and my sister did most of the talking. We both introduced ourselves and then just looked around while my sister and my wife's best friend quickly became enamoured by each other.

74

Since we weren't talking, my sister and my wife's best friend spoke for us, explaining what we did, how old we were, what we were interested in, while also actively insulting us despite us standing right there. I learned that my wife was about to start her second year of university, that she had two older sisters, that she was highly intelligent and had a thing about other people being late. As my wife and I stood awkwardly and listened, I will admit that I glanced at her every now and again, and looked from her to her friend to try and understand what the correlation might be. My first impression of her friend was that she was clearly very confident, judgemental in a way that at the time I thought was amusing, and that sure, she was pretty, but not as pretty as my wife. I thought, how quaint, I can be nice and quiet with this woman while my sister and this woman's friend enjoy the sound of their own voices. How normal and lovely and fuss-free. You could fill the Hoover Dam with how much my naive little mind didn't know.

When we got back from the barbecue (we lasted all of an hour before cochlea damage became a real possibility), I went straight to my room and my sister followed me inside. She pushed the door closed with her back and looked pleased with herself as she waited for me to ask her why she was staring at me. What? You owe me. I owe you what? I got her number. Whose number? The one you were staring at. Why? She thinks you're attractive. Did she actually use the word 'attractive'? Is she a thirty-five-year-old? Well, no. Her friend – the one who I was talking to – she told me. And how would she know that? Because her friend told her. Anyway, do you want her number or not?

I took the number, and then didn't contact her for about two weeks. I forgot about it. I was busy. But then one day I was having an argument with my sister via text about something she claimed I'd said but I definitely hadn't, and as I was searching for evidence in our previous messages, I found the number just sitting there, between two separate conversations. So I opened up a fresh message to text her.

Later my wife described the message I first sent her as cocky, but I would call it direct. I don't like wasting time, and we'd essentially learned enough about each other via my sister and her friend, so there wasn't really any need for small talk. I wrote the text in less than a minute, said *Hi, we met at the barbecue a couple of weeks ago, would you like to go out next week?* She said yes, and named a date and a place we could go, assuming I was free – I wasn't, but I made the time – and then a day later she cancelled it. And then a few hours later withdrew the cancellation. It was confusing, but it wouldn't be the strangest thing she would do at the behest of her best friend.

We dated for about two years before we got married. I was fairly certain that I wanted to marry her after about six months. Mostly because it had been six months and she'd never been late, and I didn't exhale and throw my phone across the room whenever she texted me – which was rare, the texting, because she's more of a phone-call person, says tone is often misconstrued in text messages and it bothers her. She – and her life – seemed simple and uncomplicated, calm and free of the dramatics that women I'd previously dated brought with them. Our dynamic worked: she was quietly assertive but unargumentative, happy to let me lead the way in our relationship – the opposite of my parents' relationship: dominated by my mother despite being financed by my father. My wife and I complemented each other perfectly, grew to understand what the other needed and provided it willingly, without request.

When I asked her to marry me she said yes straight away, in a matter-of-fact voice, and then later in the car half-apologised, said she had always hated the way women cried uncontrollably when men asked the question they had been expecting them to ask, particularly in public (although the public nature of the act she blamed on the men who made the choice to propose like that). She said she just wanted to say her yes and go. We were in public – at least, we were in a restaurant, but seated in a private dining room because once I'd seen her watch a public proposal on YouTube with her friend and heard them both make retching noises – and when I got down on one knee her eyes kind of flared open, which was slightly alarming, and then returned to normal.

She said yes, then put the ring on herself – she also hated the clumsy, emotional way the men struggled to put rings on women's fingers – cupped my face in her hands to kiss me, then rearranged the napkin on her lap and turned back to her cheesecake.

I had expectations of marriage, in that I expected it to be the same as when we were dating. And to a degree it has been. We still enjoy the same things, like the same kinds of experiences. The way we relate to each other hasn't changed much, except that now I refer to her as my wife and when she writes her name or types it into a form, she writes my last name. But there have been two notable differences. One is that we wake up next to each other every day, in the same bed, usually around the same time, eat breakfast across the table from each other, spend evenings together. It was an adjustment, but it came naturally and the integration was seamless.

The second is the presence of her friend. A person whose existence in her life I had previously tolerated at best, but nonetheless whose proximity I'd assumed would decrease over time as she came to understand the unspoken boundaries of a marriage she was not in, and the intimacy that she should not be a party to. But the regularity with which I see her in my house is unnatural. It started off once every couple of weeks, then once a week, then twice a week – now it's surprising if I get home from work or come out of the toilet and don't find her drinking our wine and eating our food at the kitchen table.

I expected to live with one woman when I got married. Apparently I live with two.

*

We leave the office, and I tell my assistant Bola to inform my boss that I'm working from home for the rest of the day. I hear the tail end of her saying something about a meeting someone just put in, but I do the back-of-my-hand wave thing at her, which she knows means I don't care, sort it out.

I ask my wife to follow me back home rather than the other way around, because even though she has somewhat convinced me of her ability to drive safely despite having drunk what is likely to have been at least three glasses of wine, the way she considered sitting down on the chair in my office and then decided against it told me she was unsure about her ability to get up. I ask her to be on the phone with me as we drive the twenty minutes home – and she tells me I'm being ridiculous, that actually being on the phone while driving is illegal, and I raise my eyebrows and nod at her as we get into our cars, shake my phone at her as a reminder that she pick up my call.

As we're pulling in I can't see her friend's car in the driveway – it's a silvery-grey BMW that looks like a cross between a hatchback and a saloon car that got confused about what it was supposed to be – and then I wonder if she got a taxi to the house, knowing that she would drink. Did she get a taxi here? I say to my wife over the phone. No, she drove, she replies, and hangs up as she drives past me and into her spot.

Inside I can smell salt and vinegar, clearly the flavour of the crisps they've been eating – my wife and her friend have always had a thing for it – and see our coat cupboard door flung open. She's gone home to pick up some things and get some more wine, my wife says walking past me, face inside her phone. Did she say when she'll be back? I follow her to the kitchen, where there is a breeze coming from the French doors. They have inexplicably been left open when they are usually closed, especially when there is no one in the house. We stop for a moment, both because we are aware of who has left the doors open, secure without consultation that it was neither of us, and also because there are what look like millions of crisp crumbs by the doorway, and we know who perpetrated that crime too. My wife turns to look at me, follows my gaze to the floor and the open doors, to the scuffs on the wall where her friend likely flung her shoes when she entered the house – like she always does – and finally to the open coat cupboard, and places a hand on my chest. She leaves her hand there for a few seconds as she waits for my heart to return to its resting rate and says, I'll clean it up.

Then she heads towards the cupboard where we keep the small, hand-held Hoover. Where is it? she asks. I shrug. Doesn't Angela normally leave it in here?

Angela is our cleaner, an older white woman in her early fifties who leaves boiled sweets in a small dish in the kitchen every week after she cleans, even though we've told her we don't eat them. She always replaces the old ones with new ones – we check – and leaves lavender on our pillows. Where she gets it from we have no idea, but it's always fresh. She's meticulous about her cleaning, leaves things exactly where she finds them unless she can tell they're out of place, in which case she puts them back where she knows they ordinarily go. We used her in our previous flat, just before we moved to this house, and she said she would be happy to continue cleaning for us, even though it would take her an extra thirty minutes to get here. I find her overeagerness odd. About a month ago my wife accidentally let slip that Angela was in fact recommended by her friend, which made me wonder if for the last few years Angela has been reporting details of our domesticity that my wife has not already divulged, back to my wife's friend. And although she cleans well and is generally not very nosy (other than when we're in the house at the same time and she asks us when we're going to have some little ones, to which my wife responds hours later when we're in bed, She won't see any more little ones or fives or tens or twenties if she keeps asking the same 1945 questions), I have been considering changing to a cleaner who maybe lives closer by, and who has never even visited the same Pizza Express as my wife's friend. It would be nice if at least one part of our lives was free of her friend's input and existence. Call her? I suggest. No, my wife says, it's probably here somewhere. Maybe Temi took it out to clean up a bit? I laugh because there are so many crisp crumbs by the doorway to the kitchen it looks like someone emptied a third of the bag out and stepped all over it, then used their hands to spread it around to try and make it look like it had scattered naturally. While my wife checks inside all the cupboards I step over the crumbs and notice the bottle of wine open and half-drunk on the counter, with splashes of it on the surface too. I say *the* because it's a vintage bottle that was given to us by my father when we got married, the one we were saving for a special occasion – say, the birth of a child. My wife knows the rules about that bottle because she made fun of me for it but respected my decision to save it, and she doesn't care enough about the quality of wine to even want to drink it, so I know it wouldn't have been her. She stands up straight, having found the Hoover, then follows my eyeline to the bottle on the counter. Before you say anything, she says, I did tell her. I'm sure you did, I say. I made it clear that it wasn't for regular consumption and that we were waiting for a special occasion to have it. So essentially you told her to have it. My wife rolls her eyes. You know what she's like, you tell her unicorns don't exist and she'll find a lab to create the very first one. There's still most of it left, she reasons. Half, I correct her, there's half of it left. It's wine, not world peace, rationalise your annoyance. Kim, there's people that are dying. She walks past me and leaves the kitchen to find batteries for the Hoover.

She always references the Kardashians when she thinks I'm being irrationally annoyed about something, and her quoting them irritates me more because a) she's quoting the Kardashians, b) she thinks my annoyance is irrational and c) her questioning my annoyance makes me question it too. I take a deep breath and imagine myself drinking the wine instead, and try to convince myself that I opened the bottle and just forgot that I had, that I tasted and enjoyed all of the different notes – but this is where my imagination fails, because I don't even know which notes are in it because I haven't tasted it. Then I imagine my wife's friend's face when she drank it, probably smiling to herself. She probably put some crisps in her mouth before she drank it, didn't even get the real taste. Probably almost fell over while trying to pour it and laughed as she caught the bottle before it smashed. Probably wiped the mouth of the bottle with her finger then wiped her finger on the counter. Probably swigged directly from the bottle when she realised she was too tipsy to pour it. I exhale and imagine steam coming out of my nose therefore expelling my anger. I wipe the bottle mouth, Dettol the counter and put the glasses in the dishwasher – whenever I leave them in the sink and that woman is here they get smashed; it's like a strange ritual she has where she has to break something, or someone, in this house before she leaves – then find some of the wine has splashed on to my white shirt as I was rinsing the glasses. Kim, there's people that are dying, I repeat to myself.

*

Our marriage isn't perfect, but it's better than most. We know what the other likes and doesn't like. We know when we are annoying each other and need space. We know that sometimes we will both act irrationally and that at all times one of us needs to decide to be the rational one. We know that shouting doesn't help. Thankfully my wife is not a loud or shouty person. And I can appreciate how lucky I am: I have a good job, a lovely home, a beautiful, reasonable and understanding wife, and soon a child to make us a family. But marriages are usually made up of two people, whereas I feel as though I am married to three different women. One, of course, is my wife, the woman I legally decided to marry, on purpose. The second is my wife's best friend, who is forever in our house. Her presence usually involves a few jokes at my expense, but also one or two bizarre compliments, about how I look tall today, how I look like I got dressed in daylight, or a question as to where the various rare animals I killed and sacrificed in order to cast the spell that made my wife fall in love with me are buried. Then there's the third woman, the one that I see when we've all had a bit to drink and my wife's friend has elevated the level of her insults and my wife is laughing at them and whispering with her best friend right in front of me. The third woman is completely detached from the person that I recited my vows to.

The first time I noticed it was when we were eating dinner in our half-unpacked living room a few days after we'd come back from our honeymoon. We were in the large London flat back then, not long before we moved to the suburbs. My wife and her friend were sat close to each other on one end of the corner sofa, and I was technically sat next to my wife but still a significant distance away from her. The TV was playing reruns of *My Wife and Kids* on low volume in the background, and the conversation we were having had started as a discussion of our favourite married TV couples and had somehow moved on to our favourite real-life couples. Temi reeled off a list of hers and my wife made a face, feigning offence at not being listed. Oh, but you knew that already, her friend said, drinking from one of those canned cocktails Marks and Spencer sell. My wife laughed, then she and her friend turned to glance at me and laughed again, covering their mouths like something else was going to spill out if they didn't. I mean, my wife said, then shrugged and drained the last of her cocktail, she and her friend still laughing. While my wife turned back to the TV, Temi turned to look at me for a few seconds until I became very uncomfortable and angled my body away from her and further towards the TV.

I asked my wife later, in bed, what she meant by 'I mean', and she propped her pillows up behind herself and turned to look at me. What? Earlier, when we were all in the living room, she was listing off her favourite couples and she didn't list us and you pretended to be offended and then you said 'I mean' and shrugged. Why did you do that? She picked up her book from her bedside table and opened it to the page she was on, turned it upside down on her lap, evened out the surface of the duvet cover around herself. I leaned forward to catch her eye. Yes? Yes what? she said. What did you mean by 'I mean'? She exhaled quietly and leaned back. Nothing. I meant nothing by it, it was just a joke. Always a lot of jokes about us or about me when she's around, though, aren't there? You ever noticed that? Thought about asking her to stop? By then she'd picked up her book again and turned it over, started reading, or pretended to have started reading. She dropped her wrists so the book was almost lying in her lap and began a loud deep breath but let it taper off. What would you like me to say? I've just said what I'd like you to say, to her. Okay then. I'm sorry if you feel that we have fun at your expense, it's not personal. Okay then. Okay then.

I took her apology for what it was, a way to end the

conversation and avoid explaining herself, which I also took to mean that she doesn't always want me to know why she does or says certain things. Something that reinforces the idea that she behaves differently whenever her friend is around.

When I got the call earlier from my wife and heard that woman in the background I was confused. Not because she always finds a way to be in our house. She's like a small rash that you leave untreated because you assume it will go away, but then weeks later find that it has covered your entire body. But a month or so ago my wife and I had a conversation I thought made my position clear – and the appropriate course of action – on the issue. I had been gentler in the past because I don't like arguing or any kind of confrontation, but a woman with only one university degree was regularly insulting me inside a house I paid for and taking liberties with time that could be better spent trying to have children and was instead spent drinking supermarket wine and eating non-keto-friendly foods. It was a Saturday and we were eating lunch out, my wife sipping slowly from her sparkling water. I had brought up the topic of our failed efforts to procreate and she had started drinking the water in order to avoid engaging with me about it. I think I know what our problem is. She tilted her head to one side to indicate that she was listening, so I continued. We have very little time alone. She tilted her head to the other side and grimaced as she swallowed some more water. Your friend, I began. Which friend? she said, switching back to her virgin mojito. I looked over imaginary glasses at her. Your friend, I repeated, is in our house three, four days a week, and when she comes she brings a lot of wine and because you are a good friend, you drink it with her—Studies show that alcohol doesn't necessarily—Impact fertility, I know, I said, finishing her sentence. But it's not what the wine does to your fertility, it's what the wine does to *her*. She straightened the unused fork on her left side and cleared her throat. We agree about that, yes? She nodded, reluctantly, her tongue slightly protruding from her cheek. Good. And then I fed her some words I thought would test the waters of which woman I was really married to: I can see how it makes you uncomfortable, how you want to support your lonely, single friend, but equally, you know that her 'jokes' frequently cross the line and create problems between us. There was a brief moment during which I wasn't sure I had sufficiently convinced her and had potentially done the opposite, but then she nodded again while trying to quietly chew the ice at the bottom of her cocktail glass. And that that kind of undue discomfort and stress can, I would imagine – though tell me if I'm wrong – have a negative effect on your hormones and therefore *our* ability to reproduce. Do you agree with that? She sighed and nodded again. Then after a few seconds she said, So, what would you like *me* to do about it? I picked up my napkin from my lap and wiped my mouth, then folded it and placed it behind my water glass. I think it's time to put our relationship, our future, first. And what does that require? she asked. Well, first, the holiday. We haven't spent a lot of time together and work hasn't been as busy recently, so it would be nice to actually use that time to have some date nights, go to some galleries, maybe have a couple of days in the countryside? She sighed, and then said: Anything else? Next time, the inevitable next time, she comes to our house and I'm not there, explain to her, in the language she understands, that our lives require a different set-up now, and that her visiting schedule will have to change in a significant way.

The weeks following that conversation were like living in a dream. Not only did Temi disappear, but my wife told me that she'd actually left the country entirely. The house felt peaceful for the first time in years, our time together was no longer scheduled around visits from her friend and I could come home without fear of what might be lurking in our kitchen clutching a glass of wine. For once it was just the two of us and we could finally concentrate on what was important – starting a family.

But every now and again, during those uninterrupted weeks of bliss, I would think about how the conversation with my wife had ended. After she agreed to speak to her friend and we had concluded that it was the right thing to do – with the future in mind – my wife had said: And if she says no? I downed the rest of my water and chewed my left-over ice. If she says no? We change the locks.

*

I pass my wife on my way upstairs and she holds up the hand-held Hoover again as she closes the battery slot, mutters something about how the batteries were in the bathroom and not the randoms cupboard where we keep things that don't have an obvious grouped location. A few seconds later I hear the Hoover going downstairs, and wonder if she's on her hands and knees getting all the crisps, or if she's doing her usual thing of putting her foot in the hand-hold slot and moving her leg from side to side like she's skating, because she hates bending down to use it.

Our bedroom is big, bigger than makes sense now that I think about it – even though my wife always thought it was too big, and mentioned it to me multiple times when we were discussing it with the architect. It has two large windows that look out on to the side of the house, which itself is beautifully distanced from the house next to us. The bedroom door is open and from the doorway I can see that our bed has been slept in (normal), but that it hasn't been made (not normal). On weekends my wife chases me out of the bed when I'm trying to sleep in because she wants to make it, hates the Tracey Emin-looking nature of it when it's unmade.

So it's unlikely she's left it like that on purpose, or at all, and more likely that someone else did. But before I cross the road and jump to conclusions, I think about the other possibilities, especially ones that would involve why one of my blazers is on the bed, one of the sleeves rolled up. I drop the jumper I wore to work on to the chair next to my side of the bed, and then walk back to the doorway, lean out and shout downstairs: BAAAABE. BAAAAAAABE.

What? Why are you shouting?

Did you look for the batteries in the bed?

What? Why would I look for batteries in our bed?

It's not made.

Okay . . . anything else?

Did you try on one of my blazers?

Is one of your blazers on the bed?

Yes.

I don't think I did but maybe I did.

Surely you would remember if you did?

Is it dirty?

No.

So what's the problem?

You made the bed this morning, didn't you?

I normally do, so it's likely.

Okay so why is it like that now?

Like what – can you come downstairs please, I don't want to lose my voice arguing about a bedspread and a blazer.

I take a few steps down the stairs and find her on the hall-way side of the kitchen doorway, foot still in the handhold part of the Hoover. We're not arguing, I say, hands in my pockets, leaning against the banister. The bed is like what, she repeats.

Like it's been slept in again.

What are you actually trying to ask me?

Did she sleep in our bed.

Is that a question or a statement.

Is *that* a question or a statement?

Don't be a child.

Did implies a question. She half-rolls her eyes.

She was going to sleep in the guest room when I left to come to your office, but she might have slept in our bed while I was gone.

And tried on my blazer?

And tried on your blazer.

And put the photos of us together on our bedside tables facedown?

She pauses and places her index finger gently over her lips before saying: And put the photos of us together on our bedside tables facedown. For goodness sa—, I start. Kim, she says again, there's people that are dying, we finish in unison.

After I've changed out of my shirt and attempted to wash the green-juice and wine stains out of it, I go to the study that thankfully only I have the key to. I stick it to the top of my bedside-table drawer so that no one – not even my wife – will find it. In fact she really truly does not care and never asks to come into the study or see what I'm doing in there, but it's not her I'm worried about.

I realised that I am probably more in love with my wife than she is with me before we got married, when I told her that my groomsmen had planned a week-long bachelor party covering London, Las Vegas and Lagos – the idea was that I would take three good Ls before taking the fourth that would tie me down to one woman for the rest of my life. We were walking around John Lewis, scanning things for our gift registry, and she didn't even look at me or stop walking, she just continued scanning things – without checking with me if I actually wanted them, because she wasn't interested in my opinion – and said, That sounds nice. It might involve a strip club, I said, tentatively. Okay, she said, and frowned at the price of something, then scanned it anyway. Did you hear what I said? Strip club. Yeah – you don't mind? She stopped then, and let her wrist fall slightly with the weight of the scanner in it, and turned to me. Look at me, she said, and I nodded, even though I was already looking at her. Do I look like I need to mind?

The imbalance doesn't bother me, though, because I know that our marriage isn't solely based on feelings. Its foundation is rooted in our shared desire to build and maintain a specific kind of life together. It's based on trust, honesty and the knowledge that we are in it for the long haul. So her unbotheredness isn't an issue for me like it might be for others. We have an understanding between us that I'd go as far as to say is rare.

In the study I close the door and lock it, knowing that if my wife needs me she'll likely text or call me, because as she's just demonstrated, she hates shouting between rooms/floors/walls or travelling up and down the stairs for brief conversations. The study is fairly generic-looking, with a few family photos on the walls and similar books on the shelves to those my wife suggested for my office, as well as some random sculptures. My desk is at the end of the room, right in front of the window, which I'm told is bad for my eyesight when the sun comes through it, but I have light-filtering blinds; however, I also don't tell people who critique the placement of my desk that I have light-filtering blinds, because when I think about it, let alone say it out loud, I feel my self-hatred growing. Wealth will either be hated or admired depending on how it's presented, and although I am clearly not a poor person, there are levels of obnoxious wealth that make me cautious about how I express or communicate mine.

I sit down and feel peaceful. The ambience of most of the house has long been tainted by the presence of my wife's friend and the chaos she brings to every room and situation, but this is one room she's never been inside, and never will. Every other place in the house has been polluted by some incident that involves that woman and/or something she's said. It's the reason why I've insisted we redo the two upstairs bathrooms and the library. The reason why we've had to use the downstairs bathroom for over a year. The reason why my internet history is dominated by searches about the scientific evidence behind burning sage. Those rooms have been contaminated by my wife's friend's *activities*.

*

I grew up in a relatively normal family. Two parents, two children. My older sister and I get on well enough, though I wouldn't say we're close. Our parents avoided arguing in front of us as much as possible, and though they have ideas of what they hoped our lives would be like, they never pressured us to go to a specific university, study a particular subject or go into a field that they felt was more financially lucrative. But the circles we moved in – among people of similar wealth brackets, i.e. bankers and brokers, engineers, doctors, business owners, lawyers, architects – preprogrammed into us the idea that those were the careers that bred success. We believed that a family, good career, money and connections to people who had the same would provide fulfilment. Even though when I explain this to people who work in creative industries, people who rely on their 'art' to provide them with 'happiness', they find my pursuit of wealth distasteful and a product of capitalist propaganda, I'm more than satisfied with my life. I know exactly what I want: an uncomplicated, content (because the parameters for happiness are always changing and therefore impossible to achieve) and, yes, privileged existence. And I know what it will take to get there and who I want with me on that journey. That meant knowing the traits I required in the person I chose to share that life with.

I would say I am family-oriented. I would like to have children, to go on family holidays once or twice a year, Christmases in Nigeria every now and again. I believe that women should have equal opportunities to men, equal pay and rights, free tampons – all of that stuff. Equally, I am all for being the breadwinner, and I am more than happy to be the only person in the marriage who works. I earn more than enough to do so, and thankfully, just before we got married, my wife decided that she would like the same thing. So I work and she doesn't and she gets to enjoy the fruits of my labour, something that I enjoy watching her do. I see my money as our money. She provides me with the emotional and physical support I need to go into the office Monday to Friday (and sometimes Saturday) and do my job. She asks about my day even if my work doesn't interest her, gives me back massages after the particularly bad ones, goes with me to various work and family events, doesn't ask too many questions about money and trusts me enough to handle it, rarely complains, keeps herself in great shape and avoids any kind of conflict with my family, even though sometimes I can tell it pains her not to engage them on certain topics. In turn, I provide her with the means and freedom to live the life she deserves. Our life is one of agreement and peace, but the topic of children remains a point on which we concur with differing caveats.

After my wife agreed to marry me and we'd done the engagement party and the dinner with our parents and siblings – which her friend, who was at that point of no relation whatsoever, attended – we had a discussion about our relationship. What we both wanted out of it, what us being a family would mean. She believed it would be a continuation of our current relationship, just living together. I nodded slowly, sitting on the sofa in her flat, tapping a mug of Baileys hot chocolate with two fingers. But also, building a family together, right? She sipped from her mug and look directly at me, squeezed her eyes slightly. When you say build . . . Children, I mean children. She readjusted herself on the sofa and tucked one leg under before she said, Why?

My wife's relationship with her parents is not an easy one, not one that she particularly cherishes or wants to nurture. I have noticed that when we visit them, or on the unlikely occasion that she lets them visit us, she says as little as possible, lets the conversation flow around her, only speaks when her mother or father asks her a question, to which she gives a quick answer with the specific aim of avoiding any follow-up questions. She once – in a rare display of negative emotion – said that she felt like she was their employee rather than their daughter. We'd been to their house for dinner, one of the four annual dinners her parents request, negotiated down from the original eight, and at the table her parents had reinterrogated her reasons for not working, not yet having children, not inviting some extended member of the family or other to stay in the house, not visiting them enough. Her mother in particular spoke at length about her disappointment in my wife's lack of professional accomplishments, noted that her being a housewife was nothing to be proud of, questioned what had happened to the ambitious daughter she had raised. Why did I bother paying for university for you, she said. Where was the return on investment?

If ever her mother calls her – I still think her father, who is in his mid-sixties, does not know how to use a mobile phone – she always takes it in our bedroom or our walk-in wardrobe with the door closed, standing at the back of the room so that when I press my ear to the door, I can only hear the ends of the words she's saying. I'm aware that I've had a good and pleasant upbringing, that my relationship with my parents is amicable to the point that I will call them sometimes just to check up on them and find out how they are, and that not everyone else has a relationship like that. But even my wife's friend, as obscure an individual as she is, seems to get along with her parents. Every now and again she takes a call from them when she's at our house, and though her respect for their opinions is minimal – as evidenced by her life choices (since when do Nigerians take gap years?) – she still makes a point to talk to them and joke around with them. My wife is different. She gets along with her sisters well enough, but they don't call each other. The most consistent communication between them is a WhatsApp group that largely remains dormant, save for the pictures her sisters send to mark their children's milestones. I once watched my wife respond to one of these messages with a red heart emoji before quietly exhaling as she archived the chat.

I remain confident that my wife will be a good mother. She is calm, never raises her voice, is largely unbothered by things that would deeply enrage or frustrate most people and she looks after me whenever I'm unwell or feeling physically drained. I suspect, though, that the reason she does not see family as something to build is because of her experiences with her own. She doesn't want to replicate the problems she probably does not believe she has. I did suggest therapy once, in a comment that I hoped was off the cuff enough to appear unrehearsed, to which she immediately said 'Nope', and let the 'p' echo.

I've seen the way she interacts with my family, how she

watches us at dinners, joking and laughing and engaging in normal conversation, not listing our most recent achievements in an effort to one-up one another, and I've noticed how in the car rides home she's quiet, looking out of the window and running her thumb over the knuckles of her other hand. I try to remind her – in subtle ways – that we are nothing like our parents, that we have different ideas of what we want in life, to which she always responds, You want exactly what your parents have.

*

I settle into working in the study. It's quiet, I have my noise-cancelling headphones on, and I get through a decent chunk of emails within about thirty minutes. My assistant Bola tells me that my boss came to knock on my door and was unhappy to find that I wasn't around, even though Bola had emailed my boss's assistant to explain that I would be working from home for the rest of the day, but my boss was apparently not informed. In my inbox is an email from said boss that has the subject line *Not Okay*, and contains the message: *Your asst said you went home? Not okay. Thx.*

It's about an hour or so before I feel my throat becoming dry, so I text my wife to ask if she's coming upstairs any time soon. Yes, she replies, why? I request a mug of lemon and ginger tea, and a few minutes later hear her walking

towards the door. Am I permitted to enter, she asks behind
the door, and I unlock it quickly and splay my arm out so
as to invite her in. Do you have a candle on in here? Yeah –
I point to the hazelnut candle on the windowsill – the one
your sister got me for Christmas last year. She turns her
mouth down and nods as she puts the mug on a coaster next
to my keyboard, and then she turns to me and says, Actually,
is it safe to put that there, after, you know, your shirt? She
laughs at her own joke and I smile and walk towards her,
put my arms around her waist, and she does that fake-shy
thing she does, smiles back at me and then puts her hands
on my arms – her favourite feature of mine, she once told
me – and leans in to kiss me. It starts off as a simple kiss but
then it gets slower. She puts her arms around my neck and
goes on her tiptoes like she generally has to in these situations, because she's five foot six and I'm two inches shy of
being a whole foot taller than her. I start to lift her on to the
desk, but she stops me and leans to move the mug of tea
to the other side of it, then lifts the rest of herself on to the
desk and puts one of her hands back around my neck, the
other on the side of my face, and after a few seconds, lifts
my T-shirt, then undoes my trousers – and then the doorbell rings. Not just once, but three times in a row – and we
have one of those doorbells that's from the 1900s and rings
with a shrill sound, so it's piercing and it echoes. My wife
moves me out of the way quickly – with my trousers falling

down – and practically runs down the stairs, leaving the door of the study open.

I know it's her before I even hear her voice. I know because she's the only person who rings the doorbell three times in a row when they definitely have a key, and also the only person my wife would ever run down the stairs for, despite the fact that until recently her friend was usually at our house at least two days a week and was in fact here a few hours ago. I hobble over to the door of the study, holding my trousers up, and start to close it, but stop when I hear my wife's friend say, Oh my goodness there were so many people in Tesco buying alcohol, it's like Prohibition has just ended. It's a Friday night, makes sense, my wife responds, but I was wondering if you'd been kidnapped or something, took you ages. Yeah, yeah I know, I went back to my place and then my mother called and it was a whole thing. Pele sis, my wife says. Ugh, thank you – I hear her friend kick off her shoes, and note that they've hit the wall and likely added to the scuffs she created earlier today, probably after she flung the coat cupboard doors open and left them that way, before she sprayed crisps all over the floor, after she opened our kitchen doors to invite wandering cats and other creatures in, and followed it all up by trying on my clothes and sleeping in my bed and attempting to erase my existence in my own house by placing photos of me facedown. I'm surprised she found the energy required to go anywhere after so much activity. After she has, as predicted, flung her coat back into the cupboard and checked her face in the hallway mirror and smoothed out her clothes, she turns to my wife and says: Why do you look all hot and sweaty like that? Where's the fun sponge?

I wait for my wife to say, Don't call him that, or something similar that won't put too much of a pin in the joy her friend derives from calling me names. The door is open, and she knows that because she left it that way, and the house is not one for quiet conversations, which she also knows; so she knows I've heard her friend call me a fun sponge, and granted, I'm sure she's called me worse when I'm not around, but I'm waiting for my wife to say something, anything to defend me – instead I hear them laugh, and then remember that my car is in the driveway, and that woman has been in it more than enough times to know what it looks like and to know that it being here when it wasn't before means that I am home. Then it's like my wife's friend wants to pretend it's just dawned on her and she covers her mouth with one hand, looks up the stairs and right at me – as I stand there with my trousers unbuttoned – chortles and, as my wife walks towards the kitchen, winks.

I close the door of the study quietly but can still hear the two of them – namely my wife's friend – talking and laughing loudly as they enter the kitchen that I paid for, with its marble countertops and clean lines, subway tiling and customised Smeg fridge, and picture them drinking wine that is at the perfect temperature because it lives in a state-of-the-art wine cooler that I purchased for money that bordered on obscenity. I picture them in that kitchen, which is directly below the study, laughing so much that they splutter wine against the walls, creating stains that even Angela isn't able to get out. Chewing loudly on the Snickers bars I know my wife replaces every week, brazenly leaving the wrappers in the bin so that I can see them. I picture them repeating her friend's stupid little joke for the rest of the evening and referencing it even when it doesn't make sense to, my wife making poor efforts to hide her laughter and me making every effort not to throw a perfectly good glass of wine in her friend's face. My imagination is taking on a life of its own so I stop and face the door and exhale once, twice, then one more time to check that it's worked.

On my way to being calm again, I button my trousers, put my T-shirt and noise-cancelling headphones back on, and turn the volume on the Spotify 'Music for Studying' playlist up to full, and try to recapture the ambience and focus of ten minutes ago. On my desk, the lemon and ginger tea has spilled and is pooling on the wooden floor.

*

We had a housewarming about two years after we'd moved in, because the work we wanted to do to the house took forever. I invited some friends from work, from my under-graduate degree and my masters, a few cousins I knew would be able to behave around nice things. My wife invited a selection of family friends, general friends and, of course, her best friend – who also invited whoever it was she was seeing at the time. I would call the men she dates (if that's even the correct word for it) part of a revolving door of men, but that would imply that they stick around long enough to make it through the door in the first place. In one of the only times I've ever heard my wife make fun of her friend, we started referring to them as her occasions. Men she keeps around for as long as she needs them, for social occasions to which she might be expected to bring a plus one, and instead of just taking a platonic friend, like any normal person would, feels the need to bring a man who is unaware that he is only playing the role of signifi-cant other for a few hours. A sign – I think – that despite all her protestations about marriage and monogamy and men, she actually craves the thing she demonises, and instead of admitting her true feelings, pursues the poor man's ver-sion of a relationship instead. A sad, pathetic pursuit that involves frivolous relations and retellings of stories about dates (I have overheard dozens of them) that I am a hundred per cent certain have been embellished to make her unfor-tunate little life seem more interesting than it actually is. It's one of the reasons I don't like my wife being told those

stories – they are fables made up by someone who is intel-
lectually and emotionally deficient.

Anyway, we had a housewarming party and my wife's
best friend brought this guy – he was just over six feet, so
shorter than I am at six-three. He shook both of our hands
and was complimentary about the house. My wife's friend
introduced him to us as her friend, and he gave her a play-
ful but irritated look, which I suppose is why she did what
she did later, which was to have sex with him in one of the
rooms upstairs. I know this because a friend of mine, upon
finding that the downstairs toilet (the one we were directing
people to use) was occupied, went to use one of the upstairs
bathrooms (even though we had specifically asked people
not to because – nosy). He didn't actually end up using either
of the bathrooms, because the moment he got to the top of
the stairs he could hear noises of the sexual-sounding variety coming from one of the rooms. When he came downstairs and explained this to me, he said he couldn't tell if the
noises were coming from the first bathroom, second bathroom or the library, which are all next to one another on one
side of the first floor. I couldn't understand how he didn't
know. Each of the rooms were noticeably large. After unsuc-
cessfully enquiring for a few more minutes I began to make
my way up the stairs. I was maybe eight steps from the top
when I saw the two of them looking like butter wouldn't
melt, walking across the landing and towards me. As they

passed me, the occasion of the evening patted my shoulder and said, Incredible house, and smiled. I went into the walk-in wardrobe and changed my top immediately.

Naturally I decided that we had to redo all three rooms. I didn't tell my wife why because the experience of it was disgusting enough, I didn't want to relive it. The one problem I've been trying to resolve for a while now is how to design a bathroom in which it is impossible to have sex. I've talked with architects and designers about hard edges vs soft edges, self-cleaning appliances and sensor-starting appliances. I have read more articles than makes sense about which colours are turn-offs and which colours arouse people, about shades of light that make people sad and shades of light that make people happy. I've tried pretty much everything a person could try in order to make the bathrooms and library as non-sexual as possible, but no matter which mock-ups or simulations or 3D images I'm shown, all I can see is the two of them on (or in?) the sink, the bath, in the shower, against the door (the door!), on both of the large wing-backed chairs, on the sofa, in the reading nook that sits between two shelves. Wherever it is, I see them, and it haunts me – less the image of the deed and more the idea that this woman has marked herself on this house as though marking her territory. So no matter how much it makes my wife consider having me committed, I won't finish these rooms until I stop seeing them in there – or until we can replace the offending room with something more significant, like, for example, a baby's nursery.

*

Before I got married I asked my father for some advice: if there was one thing he wished he'd known before he got married, what was it? We were sitting in his study, each holding a glass of whisky. A cigar was in his mouth, held between two teeth, unlit, because my mother had banned him from actually smoking them years ago. Well, he said, readjusting himself in his chair, one thing I wish I'd known. He took the cigar out of his mouth and sipped the whisky, gritting his teeth afterwards to manage the sharp taste. Then he pointed at me, cigar between his two fingers – Don't be like me, don't ever let a woman run your life. Once it starts, it can't be undone. I nodded in agreement and he nodded back at me. We toasted to nothing in particular and settled into silence. I cherished that piece of advice, because I felt like he was actually congratulating me on having achieved the opposite. My wife had never been controlling or interested in running my life, and he knew that. But eventually it dawned on me.

I had assumed he was talking about my relationship with my wife. He wasn't.

*

About an hour later – maybe less, because time flies when you're having fun, and the work I had to do was not enjoyable in any capacity – my wife comes upstairs and knocks on the door. I haven't locked it, so she knocks and comes in at the same time; I realise this when I feel her behind me and lift one side of the headphones away from my ear.

These headphones, which I paid good money for, are apparently no match for my wife and her friend, whose gossiping I could hear from downstairs despite the fact that they claim to be noise-cancelling. Fifteen minutes after her friend had returned I texted my wife and said: *I can still hear you gossiping even with my headphones on. Can you move to another room?* She replied four minutes later: *It's very reductive and sexist of you to assume that we're gossiping. For all you know we could be solving the economic crisis. And no, we can't, unless you would prefer red wine spilled on your cream sofa.* I squinted at my phone and reread the message to check that I'd read it correctly, remembered the last conversation we'd had about my wife's friend and her presence in the house and how my wife had agreed with me. How understanding she had been. I compared the two situations, then realised that her friend, the very creator of chaos and destruction, must have been right next to her, dictating the message to her to type out. I knew this because my wife and I had unanimously agreed that our sofa was not light enough to be cream and was in fact beige. The thought that my wife's friend was now privy even to our private text messages repulsed and enraged me. I quoted the Kardashians three times like a prayer and then resolved to move past the situation for my own sanity and to avoid prison.

Thirty minutes later I heard them both cackle, extremely loudly, and so I sent a simple, and humble – *Please*. My wife responded with *??* and I gave up, changing from the 'Music for Studying' playlist to a drill playlist to try to drown out the sound of them. And now my wife was behind me.

What? I knocked but you had your headphones on. How much longer will you be? It's then that I notice her swinging a bottle of wine, *the* bottle of wine, in one hand, a wine glass in the other. She follows my eyes to the bottle and says, I know you recorked it, but it's half-empty, and it was open for however long before anyway, so its best days are behind it. Might as well finish it? I look at her for a second, and make a conscious decision not to argue with her, so I nod and motion towards the coaster on the other side of my desk. I'm sure she sees the towel on the floor where the tea spilled a little while ago, but she doesn't say anything about it. She pours me a generous glass then squeezes my hand and says, Really sorry about the wine, again. I nod. How long d'you think you'll be working for? I shrug, mumble something about another couple of hours maybe, and she nods back and leaves the room, closing the door behind her. When I've heard her go down enough steps, I get up and lock it.

By the time I'm finishing work it's getting to six thirty. I end the day by calling my assistant for a final check-in and after I hang up I realise that I can no longer hear my wife and her friend doing whatever the non-sexist version of gossiping is. For the first time in a month, I don't like how quiet the house is.

Throughout the hours I've been working, I've also been drinking, a little bit. Just to de-stress from the day at the office and take the edge off, so to speak. At first it was just the wine my wife brought up. But after I'd finished that I remembered the bottle of whisky I kept in the study, the one my father had let me keep after the conversation about marital advice. It was vintage, he claimed, and normally I wouldn't have believed him, but the bottle even looked old – the label was raggedy and starting to peel – so I took his word for it, as well as his advice to only drink a small glass of it, and only one glass at a time, he repeated, when I was feeling reaaaally rough. I was tired, had had a trying day and my wife's friend was back inside our house. So I drank one glass of the whisky, then two, then a third half-glass – in a wine glass, not a good idea.

I go downstairs and find my wife and her friend whispering to each other in the kitchen. In one hand is my empty glass, and in the other is the bottle of whisky, now half-full. I had planned to leave the whisky upstairs, and in my mind I thought I had but I have also, somehow – maybe in an effort to keep it safe – brought it down with me. When I walk into the kitchen, my wife sits up straight and taps the table with her ring finger, then looks at me like she's just done something wrong and hopes I haven't noticed. Her friend swivels round on the chair closest to the doorway, her legs crossed over one another, one of our wine glasses in her hand, her fingers delicately around the stem, and her face smiling as though she is actually pleased to see me, the fun sponge. For a few seconds we all just look at each other, and I'm not sure what my face looks like, because I'm probably definitely a bit drunk and I hate her. My face is generally as honest as my words, so currently one must be saying what the other can't. Then I spot the empty bottle of wine on the counter, and even though I'm aware that I'm the one who helped finish it, I'm still annoyed that I'm not the one who opened it in the first place, and I'm sure she catches me looking at it, because then she swivels towards the counter where it's sitting, then back to me, and says, Sorry-o.

*

I hate a lot of things about my wife's friend, but the thing I hate most is that, more and more, she makes me look twice at my wife.

At this point, we've eaten countless meals together, some-times amicably discussing banal topics like which Korean restaurant does the best bibimbap, sometimes while I watch TV and the two of them talk over it, but more during her last few visits, a lot of the discussions turned to the past and her friend began to share anecdotes I hadn't heard before, or a like or dislike my wife has that I was unaware of.

Once, as my wife and I got ready for a date night, her friend sat in our bedroom drinking a glass of champagne for no good reason, and retold the story of a night out during our university years when my wife had apparently been so drunk that she'd crashed her friend's car into a parked car. She gesticulated wildly as she spoke, and I watched her glass carefully as she jerked her arms about to illustrate the abso-lutely hilarious nature of the story. She used phrases like 'the way you always do' and 'you know how we used to'. She wanted to make it clear that this was a life, and a version of my wife, that existed before me. These stories always involve antics that are not prescriptive to the person I'm married to. Words said that sound nothing like her, emotions that I've never seen her express, decisions made that are in complete contrast to the ones my wife would make now, and though I am aware that this is a concerted effort by her friend to make me question my knowledge of my wife, to establish that she knows my wife better than I do, I still watch my wife's responses to these stories. She always laughs, never disputes them, occasionally lets slip that she wishes she could relive these moments and then flashes a nervous look in my direction, almost like she's forgotten I'm there. Then her friend will look at me, smile like someone who's just fired you but used the phrase 'a mutual parting of ways', and sip whatever happens to be in her hand.

*

I keep my eyes on my wife's friend as I walk over to the sink and rinse out my wine glass before going to sit by my wife, and keep watching as she pours me a glass of wine. I drink as my wife's friend smiles at me, says, I got that one from Tesco, not quite like yours but it's still nice, right? I consider spitting it out, but let myself swallow it, grimacing slightly to clearly communicate that it is not nice. Tastes like it's from Tesco too. My wife raises her eyebrows at my comment and turns back to her own glass of wine, almost puts her face inside it. Her friend opens her mouth like she's about to say something, so I pre-empt her: No work today? She closes her mouth to smile again as she rotates her wine glass on the table. No, I just . . . didn't feel like being in the office today. She picks up her phone from the table and shakes it. I can reply to emails from this if I need to. Do you know what this is? Moh-bile phoh-ne. Means you can do things while mobile. Mobile means able to move freely and easily.

My wife splutters quietly but enough for me to notice. Her friend continues speaking. And work isn't everything, you know? Like I love my job, being able to run my own company, work from anywhere. But sometimes it's just nice to take some time out to be with the people who really matter, like friends – she makes grabby hands towards my wife, who laughs – and friends who are like family – then she taps a finger on the table towards me. It's been too long, hasn't it? I refuse to answer this and swig from my wine glass instead, which tastes like someone juiced a potato, added some expired grapes and called it wine.

You know, she continues, if you ever manage to successfully – she nods towards my crotch – have a baby, you can't work so much. My friend here will really need you to be a supportive husband and father. I start to interrupt but she continues, raising her hand to stop me speaking. I am distressed by my own obedience when I do. I know, she says, I know what you're going to say, that you'll step up when the time comes. But darling, she says, and at that I down my glass, and retch quietly at the taste, you can't wait until then to be the man that she needs you to be. It's got to be right now, you know? You can't wait for the baby to be here before becoming that man. She bursts into laughter and my wife does too, and I remember then that they've been drinking all day, and I'm very much behind. I look at my watch and wonder if it would be acceptable to kick her out, or if I should ask my brother-in-law – my sister's husband, who is also the brother of my wife's friend, who I know does not like his sister almost as much as I don't (we bonded over this shortly after he started dating my sister) – to text his sister and say that their parents have been in a car crash, just to get her to leave. Although knowing her, she would probably glance at the text, lock her phone and then continue drinking.

*

I pictured our life like this: we date for a little while, we get married at a ceremony in which none of our relatives give out wedding paraphernalia with our faces on it. After a few years of travelling, we have children – three, to be exact. The middle child will fulfil the stereotype of being the weird middle child, but in the child-genius kind of way. Our children avoid hanging out with the two of us together because they hate how affectionate we are. I become one of those men that I see women zooming in on on Instagram, the Black men with the salt-and-pepper hair and beards, but faces like they're still thirty-four. Later in life, let's say our early forties, my wife tells me she wants one more child. It surprises me – in fact, I try to talk her out of it, but she's adamant – one more will complete the family, she says, and she's healthy and I haven't quite decided what she'll be doing during the day when I'm at work, but it will probably have something to do with clothing and charity. We'll have the fourth child, but then by some freak act of genetics, it's twins. Twins don't run in either of our families and for years people will joke that my wife cheated, but we both know she doesn't care enough to do that.

One of our kids will be interested in my work at first and then split off to do something techy that we will always ask them to explain when they visit. The weird middle child will work in medical research and always have those little marks and impressions around their eyes from wearing medical goggles all day. The third will become a teacher or professor, which will shock us all because they seemed the most interesting of the kids and teaching never really seemed on the cards for them. Of the twins, one will become an actor, which will make perfect sense because they have always been very dramatic and able to repeat things we've said verbatim after hearing them only once, weeks and months ago. The other twin will take a little while to decide what they want to do, but when they decide it'll involve politics and the UN and travelling almost every week, and my wife and I will be grateful that the other kids gave us grandchildren because clearly this one was never going to be in one place long enough for that.

I pictured two houses in this country, one flat. The first house will be on the outskirts of central London, driveable distance, walkable if you're into that sort of thing. It'll have enough rooms for all the kids, but a few spare guest rooms for when they come with their kids. The kitchen will be bigger than the one we have now, with a walk-in pantry: my wife doesn't care about this, or anything interiors-related – a running joke between us that she is actually a stay-at-home husband and I am the working wife – but I saw it on a home improvement show once and now I have to have it. All the surfaces in our house will be perfectly unarousing; no one will have sex on them, ever. In fact our children will remain chaste until marriage, and once they're married they'll only ever have sex in their own beds and not in other people's houses.

I pictured the other house being somewhere like Brighton where there is more direct exposure to the sun and you can walk down to the beach. I pictured some sprightly interior designer in large round orange glasses helping us to accessorise the space with a lot of bright colours that we will later regret agreeing to. I pictured us with one of those walls that parents mark their children's height on, the two of us commiserating when the first of our children grows taller than me. I pictured the flat in central London, on one of those streets where it is impossible to find reasonably priced public parking.

I pictured us fighting over things like where the children want to go to university, whether or not they can have friends of the opposite sex over in their rooms with the door closed;

my wife won't mind, I will. I pictured us spending summers in Italy and South Africa, Christmases in Nigeria, Easters in Amsterdam with my favourite cousin who lives there.

I pictured us being one of those couples who are reminded one day that they've been married for over thirty years and look at each other, surprised, and laugh – How did *that* happen? I pictured us content, rather than happy, because in reality, happiness is an unachievable concept designed to keep people unhappy and spending money on things they don't need. I pictured us sitting in the library together, a cup of coffee in my hand (not keto-friendly because by then we've dispensed with that idea), a tea of some variety in hers, probably jasmine.

I pictured a life of upscale simplicity. A life in which we achieve the things we set out to achieve, we get what we want without disturbing other people's peace. A life with family who are interested and invested in our lives but not nosy and invasive. A life in which we are not a couple who do pregnancy announcements or post pictures of our children on the internet but with their faces blurred because that's just as obnoxious as posting pictures of them at all. A life with friends who have lives of their own, other friends of their own, minds of their own. A life without her.

She is in many ways similar to my sister – too talkative, overopinionated, often rude, nosy, unappreciative, late, argumentative, conceited, selfish – so in theory, I should be able to manage her. But she is so much worse than my sister, in every possible way. I once thought she might be a doting aunt to our children, someone to keep my wife company whenever I went away for business. Someone with whom I would plan my wife's birthday or a surprise trip for her – for both of them to go on – just because. Someone who I would ask to come over when my wife wasn't feeling like herself, needed some time with her best friend. I wonder every now and again if the life I pictured for us is still possible, if my wife might one day come to her senses and get rid of this friend and replace her with a different, better one.

But then I also wonder if my wife would be the same person without her friend in her life. Does one exist without the other? Are they intrinsically linked in more than one way? Is my wife a more docile version of her friend dialled down by marriage and performed domesticity, just one hair trigger away from becoming her? I have to ask myself more often than not these days, at the beginning, middle or end of her friend's visits, whether all that's now left to restore balance to our world is her permanent removal. It's never got to the point of hiring a hit man or buying poison, but once, after maybe our worst argument, I did call a few head-hunters and tell them about her. During a visit to our house a few days later, I heard her mention to my wife that she'd been receiving calls from random companies about jobs in

Jakarta and Beijing. But how would I survive in China without my best friend? she'd said, leaning her head on my wife's shoulder.

*

Before I speak I imagine my wife's friend choking slightly on the wine in her mouth, coughing and then touching her hand to her head, realising she doesn't feel well and deciding that she needs to go home. I think the baby thing is really a matter between husband and wife, I say, opening a bottle of red that has no sentimental value whatsoever, and pouring myself a large glass. I recork the bottle and place it next to myself, the furthest point away from my wife's friend. She shrugs, makes a face like she doesn't consider what I have said to be important. But there's that saying, though, isn't there, something about a village. My wife fills in the gaps – It takes a village to raise a child. Right, right, her friend says. So really, that conversation might exist between the two of you, but the reality of it – you know, who you call to babysit last minute, who you ask to do the pick-up from school when you're both busy— What's funny? I sip some wine and shake my head, raise my palm to get her to continue, though I'm still laughing. My wife smiles at me even though I don't think she knows what I'm laughing at. No please, you first, her friend says. Just – the bit where you said 'who you call to babysit', it kind of sounded like you were thinking of yourself. I pause to laugh before continuing, But then I thought that couldn't be right because, well, you know, we have no plans to call you to babysit. My wife splutters but turns it into a cough, and I rub her back to aid her cover-up. Her friend takes a moment to look at me, then at my wife, then at the bottom of her wine glass, which is almost empty. Could you pass the wine please, she says to me, and after I pause for a significant amount of time – like I needed to compute her request and have it approved by the administrator – I do. After she's finished the wine in her glass and then also poured herself a large glass of the red I just opened, she puts the cork next to her left arm – as far away from me as possible – and places the bottle in the middle of the table. To an extent, she says, sipping, you're right. It would be impossible to babysit for a child that doesn't exist. My wife covers her mouth before abruptly pouring some wine down her throat and then beginning to pour herself another glass of wine from the bottle in the middle of the table. She starts to pour quite quickly, generously, until she notices that both her friend and I are watching, and then she stops pouring. A half-glass.

*

My wife has only ever intervened when it comes to her friend once. She asked me to apologise. Her friend had ruined our long-planned anniversary dinner by coming over and pre-tending to be upset about a man I was sure I'd heard her refer to as being more generic than a Tesco bag, and I had asked her when she was going to leave. The conversation had morphed into an argument about how I was somehow being insensitive by asking her to leave. Her friend had cried silent, apparently emotive tears and my wife had looked at me, one of those looks that says, You're sleeping on the sofa, but I knew I wasn't wrong, so that night I got into the bed I paid for, with money I earned, in the house I also paid for.

My wife turned away from me in said bed, and asked me to apologise. I asked her to repeat herself because I was sure I'd misunderstood. Apologise for what? I don't recall saying anything that requires an apology. Then she turned to look at me. You don't 'recall' telling her that she should disappear? I was on my side facing her, and then lay on my back to stare at the top left corner of our four-poster bed. I don't recall saying it because I didn't say it. I just asked her to leave. I turned to face her again. She said nothing for a few seconds and then turned to lie on her back and stare at a spot in the top left corner of the bed. She opened her mouth to speak and sighed. Don't worry about it, she said, then turned away from me and switched off her bedside lamp. We didn't talk about it afterwards, and in the morning she acted like noth-ing had happened, behaved as normal. But I could tell she had told her friend about it, because the next time she came over and my wife wasn't in the room she raised her glass and winked at me.

*

My wife's friend declares herself hungry and asks when the food is going to arrive. I explain that I haven't ordered it yet because I was going to do it at work, then I came home and I was, you know, working, and found it particularly difficult to concentrate with all the background noise. So will we starve today or will you order it after the monologue? I smile a smile that I hope communicates how much I despise her and take out my phone to order. I'm guessing you want the same food as before? My wife says yes and her friend says, I don't know, you know, I'm thinking maybe I'll get some gyoza or something. Can I see the menu again? She holds her hand out as though to receive my phone. I lean back, pull my body as far away from her as possible even though she's sat at the opposite end of the table to me. I tell her the name of the restaurant. Don't want me to see your texts to your girlfriends? she says. My wife doesn't flinch, and instead they look through the menu on her phone and my wife recommends the vegetable gyoza and teriyaki chicken. I watch them as they make a mountain out of a molehill, picking at every little thing each item on the menu has or doesn't have. They debate the amount of sauce you get with the teriyaki chicken and the portion size, the number of gyoza in a single portion and how much soy sauce they give you with them. They even discuss the fact that the soy sauce we have in the house isn't as nice as the soy sauce you get from restaurants. They also debate whether or not to order Coke or lemonade from the restaurant, because we have some spirits in the cupboard that we never drink. Then they have a five-minute conversation in which they reminisce about the last time they mixed wine and spirits, and they conclude that it's probably better for them not to get Coke and lemonade to mix with the spirits, and that if we run out of wine – which we won't because our wine cooler is still nearly full and there are some cases in the basement – they (at this point each probably one or two bottles down) will drive to Tesco and buy some. It's strange observing my wife being so granular about ordering food – whenever we order out and it's just the two of us, she asks what the special of the day is and says she'll just have that.

At least ten minutes pass. Okay, my wife's friend says, clapping her hands together and placing them under her chin. We've decided. Excellent. As they read out their orders to me I realise that they're identical, except that my wife's is gluten-free, in a nod to healthy eating. I input my wife's order first and then hover over the buttons to double each dish and decide against it. I order some noodles and gyoza for myself and a bit of sushi along with three extra sachets of soy sauce. I briefly consider the ramifications of not including my wife's friend's order and dismiss them. The look on her face alone will be worth it. I imagine her frantically searching through the bags and then diving for my neck like a mad-woman. I think about setting up a hidden camera and then decide against it. The memory will be enough.

My wife is sitting next to me but her chair is facing slightly away from me so while we wait for the food to arrive I run my fingers from the nape of her neck to the middle of her back and up again. Her friend, who I know hates any form of affection between us, notices this and starts to interrogate me with questions: What did you order? Yakisoba and gyoza and some sushi. That's a lot, isn't it? Yep. You're gonna have to cut down on that when you have kids, otherwise you'll be rolling after your kids not running after them, y'know? We're only having one, I say matter-of-factly, and she pretends to look taken aback. Oh, I assumed you'd have more. My friend did mention you were planning on one, but you know how it goes, right? You have one and then the husband says, Ahh let's have one more, this one is so cute, and the wife is looking at her body thinking absolutely not, but you know women are trained to make men happy so she says yes, and after that he's supposed to get the snip but he does a Michael Kyle and he doesn't, then there's baby number three and twelve years later you resent each other because it wasn't even her idea to have kids in the first place! But, you know, I'm sure you guys are different, you both mutually came up with the idea to have kids, didn't you? No, my wife says. His idea, remember? But we both agreed, I cut in. No one is being forced. Her friend swirls the wine around in her glass before taking what looks like a tenth of a sip. Well, she says, you'll need to make sure you're done with the construction site upstairs first. If he can ever figure out what he wants, my wife says and finishes the rest of her glass, swiftly pouring herself another. I don't say anything, and instead a look passes between my wife's friend and me – something between shared acknowledgement and mutual hatred – and then she smirks while almost dipping her face into her glass to drink from it, downs it and says, Honestly, you're wasting so much money tinkering up there. Think of all the starving children who could do with that money you're spending on renovating. Think of the waste, the time, the environmental impact. She puts her empty glass down and places her hands under her chin again like she's talking to an insolent child. But you don't think about any of that, do you? I just don't understand how you expect to figure out fatherhood when you can't even decide how to renovate a few rooms that didn't even need renovating. I hold the wine in my mouth for a moment as I consider my options. Their little alliance is getting on my last nerve, and I swallow before speaking. Well, I've been trying to figure out other 'impactful' things first. She scoffs, Like what? Like which room you contaminated. Can't have my child sleeping in a tainted room now, can we?

ORE AGBAJE-WILLIAMS

Her eyes widen for just one split second and it's all the reaction I need. She keeps her eyes on her wine glass as she brings it to her mouth, and then my wife asks what I mean by 'contaminated'. Her friend says, I have no idea what he's talking about. I pour a significant amount of wine down my throat and grit my teeth as I swallow it. Yes you do, I say, lowering my head slightly to look at her like *she's* an insolent child. I really don't, she says, sipping again. Honestly, not a clue. What are you talking about? So she wants me to say it. I look from her to my wife, who seems genuinely confused and interested in what will happen next, what I'm about to reveal.

She had intercourse in one of the rooms upstairs during our housewarming.

My wife splutters and this time wine goes across the table. I make to go and get some napkins but my wife puts a hand on my arm and goes to get them herself, laughs after she's able to swallow the remaining wine in her mouth and asks me to repeat myself. I do. After she's wiped the table she looks at her friend, shock and amusement on her face. You had sex in one of the bathrooms? Or the library, I interject. Oh wow, the library too? No, in one of the rooms, I just don't know which. My wife swivels her chair to face me. Wait. Hold on. Is that why you're redoing all those rooms, because you don't know which one she had sex in? I nod, and down the rest of the wine in my glass. She turns to her friend and probes her with questions, all of which her friend shrugs at. My wife laughs throughout, as though the concept of her friend engaging in coitus in our house is a source of entertainment. Just ask her which room she did it in, she says to me eventually, and then adds, Also, no one says intercourse, it's not 1960, you can just say the word 'sex'. I look from my wife to her friend and back to my wife. Okay, ask her then, I say to my wife. No, you ask her, she says. Fine, I say, turning to her friend. Was it one of the bathrooms or the library? She smiles inside her glass and puts it down on the table slowly, so that it doesn't make a sound. My wife and I are watching her.

Who says it was one of those rooms?

Three

Look, all good things come to an end. Good films, good food, good clothes, good books, good friendships, below-average marriages. While to some I may be desecrating the sanctity of marriage – though I doubt the sanctity of marriage still exists because, I mean, look at the divorce rates – I truly believe that at the end of all this, both my friend and her husband will be happier. He will see that the woman he married is simply an apparition of the person she thought she had to become, and she will see that the life we planned for ourselves is truly the one she wants. This man, my friend, this marriage, was never going to last. Ultimately I think she knows that. I think that maybe she's been waiting all this time for me to save her again, like I did that day in the changing room at school. But I think she's sat too comfortably on the periphery for longer than is fair.

*

Here is the abridged version: I grew up with a lot of money and have been accustomed to a specific kind of lifestyle ever since. The first time I rolled my eyes at my father I was six, and he told me I reminded him of his sister who was divorced and alone. When I was seven my mother started making me get plates of food for my father at family gatherings – finally I asked if he had broken his legs and she asked me if I had heard myself correctly before pinching the back of my neck and telling me that I should be grateful that we were in a public place. I decided unfiltered honesty was the best policy when I turned eleven. I have disliked overtly strong scents ever since a boy who appeared to bathe in Lynx body spray asked for my number at a school dance. I strongly believe that if someone is telling a funny story and it takes longer than fifteen seconds for the set-up the punchline is unlikely to be worth waiting for. Ever since I was moved up a year at school I have had an unwavering belief in my superiority. I can only live in homes with at least two full bathrooms. I haven't flown economy since I was ten years old. Once, a man at a bar told me I looked like the mother of his children so I registered him as a sex offender online. When we were sixteen my friend and I used her older sisters' IDs to get tattoos at a parlour next door to where my oldest brother got his hair cut. He gave us a lift and paid for the tattoos because I found condoms in his coat pocket and used them as leverage to strike up a beneficial deal. The tattoos are of our initials.

Hers is a T, barely half a millimetre in size, behind her ear. I believe that anyone who claims to have more than one best friend is a pathological liar. I also believe that women who call their husbands or partners their best friends or better halves should be imprisoned. I can list all my friends on two fingers: my friend, and my sister-in-law. The latter has a poor alcohol tolerance but is happy to spend her husband's money so our shopping trips are enjoyable. She has since moved to Nigeria, though, and no shopping trip is worth that long a flight. I truly believe that if I decided to, I could make anyone like me. I have a talent for getting people to believe anything I say. I have read numerous highly regarded journals that have gathered scientific data to prove that men are evidence of an anatomical mistake.

*

What? he says. He is blinking a lot, like he is struggling to sharpen the image of me in front of him. Nothing, I say, and watch my friend drink slowly from her glass to avoid either of us seeing her face. No, no you said something about the room it was in. I shake my head as I swirl wine around in my glass and watch as it moves closer to the edge. He stares at me for a few seconds, then looks back at his glass, searching for an intelligent thing to say, but as in most things, he remains lacking. Well, this is awkward, I say, I think you've got confused. There was a *lot* of alcohol being passed around the house that evening, though, so completely understandable that you've misplaced the facts – don't even worry about it. I won't hold it against you. You're only human after all! I smile and raise an impromptu toast – To a lack of evidence! My friend laughs and her husband does not join in the toast, sipping his wine instead. If he keeps drinking at this rate, he'll soon be slurring his words.

When she realises he's not laughing, my friend turns to her husband. For a moment they look directly at each other and I watch her smile disappear.

*

Earlier this afternoon, as my friend left to go and play Sylvanian Families with her husband, I discovered two deeply distressing things.

They were in, of all places, the bathroom. I am a firm believer that you can tell a lot about a person by looking at the contents of their bathroom. There are items that expose them, their internal and external ailments, their bizarre bathing practices, their questionable skincare choices. Their teeth-whitening strips and their decision to use tampons without applicators (barbaric). Over the years I've observed many things about my friend and her husband by way of their bathroom, including the fact that even though they can afford to replace their Aesop hand soap and moisturiser with new bottles, they actually refill them with Dove handwash and Baylis & Harding moisturiser, which they hide in the cupboard. Confirmation that rich people really are the cheapest people on earth. The contents of their cupboard never really change, and I know my friend and her skincare habits like the back of my hand, so I never check it any more, and bored of the subpar pillows in their guest room, I entered the bathroom purely intending to check my lipstick. I am clinical about my lipstick and the wine drinking had dulled it. I used a tissue to correct it and when I pressed the pedal bin to throw away the tissue, I saw a pregnancy test at the top of the pile of waste. It was negative. My initial response: how strange that someone would visit this house and do a pregnancy test here rather than in the privacy of their own home. My second response: recalling my friend's suspicious behaviour earlier on the phone to our mutual sister-in-law: lack of eye contact, mumbled replies, awkward earring fiddling. My third response: rapidly searching the rest of the bathroom for further evidence to corroborate what I had just seen. I tried to reason with myself – people only take pregnancy tests if they think they're pregnant. People only think they're pregnant if they believe that they have engaged in activity that could result in pregnancy. Yes, she mentioned eons ago that her in-laws were desperate for her to have a baby, and yes about a month ago she mentioned that they were going to start *trying*, and yes her cancellation of our annual holiday would now make sense if they really were trying but this is also the woman who once handed her own niece back to her sister because she found the concept of a miniature human unnatural. The woman who googled 'how to get your tubes tied' after we watched a video of a woman giving birth in Biology. I had imagined that she was *trying* in as much as she *tries* not to schedule anything at the same time as the quarterly dinners with her mother and father she agreed to. But this was different. There was a used pregnancy test in a home that I frequent more than most. This was either a sick joke for which I could congratulate my friend later, or a just-in-case test for a late period. Either way I would not let myself conclude that there was any other explanation. I had to find the evidence I needed to know she was neither pregnant, nor was she trying to be. I opened the cupboard, the contents of which I had convinced myself never changed. Lo and behold, next to a very full container of shaving cream that had definitely never ever been used, was a half-empty bottle of prenatal vitamins.

*

In friendship I find knowledge. Knowledge of who a person is, what motivates them, how they spend their time, their likes and dislikes. For example, how they hate the sound of forks against teeth, or when men pull chairs out for them. How it makes them want to take a life when the film is starting in the cinema and someone under the age of twenty is still scrolling through their ex's Instagram or rewatching their own Snapchat story. Things like how they keep receipts from all the clothes they buy until the return period ends, just in case they find a suspicious-looking stain or a loose thread. That they are physically repulsed by the sound of polystyrene and love the sound of wine being poured into a glass. That they once went to the doctor because they started to itch whenever their mother called and they thought that maybe they were allergic to her. Or that their husband – in addition to yawning multiple times – always unconsciously says Yes, yes goodnight, just before he falls asleep. You know the big things and little things, the things that are insignificant and the things that make them who they are, like what they want from life and what they don't. You know the way they felt when they went to university and discovered what it was like to be unshackled from expectation for the first time. To become whoever they decided that evening required, to finally tell people what they really thought instead of making themselves quieter, less visible. To know how it feels to ghost a man and feel the power of rejecting someone pulsing through their veins, to try on strength and outspokenness for size and realise that it fits them perfectly. You remember the phone call during which they told you, I just told a man that I was a French actress and here for the semester researching my next role and he said he didn't realise there were Black people in France. You remember when they got kicked out of a Ralph Lauren shop for telling a woman that she could purchase the same top for less than seventy-five per cent of the listed price at the TK Maxx a five-minute walk away. You remember the moments that allowed them to see their potential, their own capability to enjoy life. You are the person who believes in them and helps them to pursue their goals, to achieve the life that you know they deserve. You are the person who knows them best.

I knew when I knocked the deodorant out of my friend's hand on purpose – I noticed her being precious about it and putting it back in the box (who keeps the box?) after every use – that she was the child of controlling Nigerian parents and that we would become best friends. I knew she was just like me, though her situation was worse, but that there was time for her to be saved, and my role was to be her saviour. We were both Nigerian, both girls, both expected to study something along the lines of law, medicine, accounting or engineering, and also to find a nice Nigerian boy, marry him, pop out some babies and raise them, all while maintaining high positions in our careers. It was thought, I'm sure, that we would become like our mothers, fix plates for our fathers and uncles at family events, continue the tradition of plucking our eyebrows into obscurity and then drawing them on with kohl pencils made for eyes not eyebrows; and like our mothers, spread fake news throughout every and any group chat in which we might find ourselves, and respond to any other fake news – whether it be about WhatsApp stealing your bank details (it doesn't), how Apple is making a phone that can read your mind (also not true), or how your phone is listening to you (this is actually true) – with a *thank you my sister*, followed by two prayer-hand emojis. Yet we've both strayed – in our own ways. I refused to get married. My parents paraded men in front of me, and some men paraded themselves – but every encounter I have had with them, my own father and brothers included, has shown me how fickle they are. Men are instruments, not partners. Their presumed superiority over women throughout history has made them complacent and stopped them from adequately evolving, and so now they are no longer fit for long-term use. They serve a purpose and then they expire, and I need the excitement of new shiny things at least once a month, if not every two weeks. And my friend, she doesn't work, didn't have children the moment she said 'I do', and I have never seen her use a pot or pan since she got married. What's more, I see her face when I make a joke about her husband, about the way he chews, or speaks, or dresses, or gets annoyed. I can see the smile peek at the sides of her mouth, then make its way up to her eyes. She enjoys the fun of it as much as I do, and that's why, even with the ring on her finger and the change to her last name, I believe that she still wants that life we talked about as quietly rebellious teenagers just as much as I do.

Recently, though, I've been worried that she's slowly regressing back to the child she used to be, a woman who is silent and subservient. Sometimes it's like I'm watching a Stepford wife developing in front of my eyes. I look at the way she dresses, the way she sits and waits for someone to tell her what is going to happen next. Every now and again I wonder if during her quarterly visits, my friend's mother has been microdosing her with some submission formula while simultaneously threatening to cut me out of her life, because the transformation has been so disturbing it can only have been brought about by something extreme. But our friendship is sacred and important, and I have to hold out hope that she's still in there, that she just needs a little reminding.

*

When the food arrives my friend's husband makes a beeline for the kitchen sink to wash his hands while my friend goes to the door to collect it, so I go to the downstairs bathroom.

I step on the pedal of the bathroom bin to check that the test is still there and still negative, and then flick some water on my face to remind myself of my purpose. I check the cupboard again for the prenatal vitamins and find them where I left them, next to the shaving cream. In my state of shock earlier I didn't investigate them fully, but now I pull them out and read the label: medical speak medical speak medical speak and also great for women TTC. I sound out the acronym a few times before realising it means 'Trying to Conceive'. I turn the bottle around in my hand a few times and look closely at the number of tablets it claims to have originally contained. One hundred and twenty tablets, and at least half of them are already gone. I do the maths. Clearly she has been taking these vitamins for more than a month. I consider whether my recollection of when she told me they started trying is inaccurate and then remember that I have a perfect memory. I consider every scenario that involves her not lying to me. We don't do that. We are not those people. We are best friends. I repeat the words like a mantra as I replace the vitamins next to the shaving cream in the cupboard. I look at myself in the mirror and talk quietly to my reflection. It's fine. She's not pregnant. Darkness. Light. Remember.

When I return to the kitchen my friend is searching through the bags as though she's lost something, and her husband is already eating his food. I find myself looking at her stomach again as I walk towards her and exhale when I can see her top billowing.

She's still rifling through the two bags – despite one of

them being empty – when I ask her where my food is and she shakes her head. What are you looking for? She stops then, and laughs. What? She puts her hands on the table and leans forward, smiling as she looks at her husband, who it is now clear has been practising his nonchalant face. He raises his eyebrows halfway up his forehead and glances quickly to the side and then back to his food.

I will commend him for one thing, and that's that he went to the effort of forgetting my order, a move I would have made if I had not yet gone through puberty. But for him, for someone of his mental capabilities, it is an achievement. For maybe fifteen seconds, I respect him. My friend, organised as ever, reads through the receipt, double-checking that what she thinks has happened has in fact happened. She rereads it and comes to the realisation that my dishes are missing. She asks her husband, Did you order Temi's food? He's up getting another set of chopsticks when she asks, so we wait until he turns back to face us and returns to the table for his response: She asked for the teriyaki chicken and vegetable gyoza, right? My friend looks at me, and I nod, and she nods back to him. Well, we have one vegetable gyoza and one chicken teriyaki. Yes but those are mine, they're gluten-free, she says. He shrugs and uses his chopsticks to put a piece of chicken gyoza in his mouth.

I know he expects me to be annoyed, maybe even angry or upset, so instead I say, No worries, and enquire as to whether or not he thinks he'll be able to finish his gyoza and chicken yakisoba. He stops halfway through putting a second piece of gyoza into his mouth and looks at my friend, who looks back at him pleadingly and who I imagine expects some level of kindness from him. He goes to a cupboard close by and brings out a bowl, puts some of his noodles and one piece of gyoza in it, and balances a pair of chopsticks on the side of the bowl, pushes it towards me. It should be enough, I think to myself. I should be careful about how much I irritate him, considering that it's only just seven o'clock, but then I think about the items I discovered in their bathroom. I move closer to him and generously lift one more piece of gyoza out of the plastic container and place it in the bowl, then add three or four more of the noodles, then push the bowl towards him, and pull the rest of the gyoza, noodles and the entire container of sushi towards myself. The best part about the entire exchange is that he watches me do all of it, and in fact lifts his hands in order to make room for me to do so, staring as the rest of his food walks with me to the other end of the table, his wife sitting silently, observing, Switzerland between us.

*

When she told me that she and her husband were trying for a baby we were outside a café not far from my flat. She'd asked to meet me, which in itself raised alarm bells. Normally one of us would simply say: I'm at [insert location here] and the other would arrive no more than twenty minutes later.

The weather was attempting summer, but there was still that awkward chill and aggressive wind so I was wearing a thicker coat; my friend, knees together at the table, a scarf around her neck and her ring finger tapping against her mug, was bundled up in one of those coats from the place in Oxford Circus that always gets protested by the activists with fake blood. I sat down and she smiled, asked how I was, which we also never do, because we just declare how we are to the other person. I told her I was fine and asked if she was getting a divorce. She cocked her head to one side and said, No, but—Wait, I said, I want to order a drink so I can spit it out dramatically and act surprised when you tell me that you've decided to become swingers instead. She smiled again. We are, she paused while a waitress delivered a slice of lemon tart to our table with two forks, going to have a baby. I didn't react, so she continued. I think she thought I was going to ask if she meant she was pregnant, but I can usually tell when people are pregnant, and knew she wasn't. We're going to start trying, I mean. I sat back and crossed my arms, nodded slowly. And this is what you want? She opened her mouth to answer but didn't realise the question was rhetorical, so I continued before she was able to. You want a little person in your pocket, in your bed, in your bank account, in your house, in your ear, in your wardrobe, in your kitchen, in your remodelled bathrooms? You want that? She gave me a closed-mouth smile.

It was difficult to see my friend, this wise and beautiful woman, fall in love – or something adjacent to that – with this ... person, without questioning whether her goals – which we once shared – had changed. Was she the same person who retched at public proposal videos with me, who'd had a crush on my oldest brother until the day she watched him trip up a kerb and felt the bile rise up her throat?

I realise that having someone, someone to love and share your life with, is a nice thing to have. That physical companionship is, of course, nice. But the concept of romantic happily ever after has become increasingly alien to me, and I know it isn't necessary for survival. And for those desperate to procreate and produce someone whose youth they one day will be jealous of, there are bone marrow studies which show that men are not imperative to the survival and growth of the human race. I am one hundred per cent positive that my friend would be happier, and better off mentally, physically, and even financially – his pay cheque is satisfactory but I have seen and personally experienced better – without her husband. Yet there she was in front of me, telling me that they were about to try and have a baby.

I wanted to understand but the understanding evaded me. The reasoning for wanting to have a child evades me. Why would you willingly invite an alien being that sucks the life from you into your body, house it for months, then once it has violently ejected itself from your body, continue to support it for at least eighteen more years? Why would you want to shoulder the emotional burden of another person and have to teach them how the world works? When you could just get a dog and be done with it?

Why now? I asked. She shrugged. It's been a while since we got married. Yes, thirty-five seconds. It's been over three years. Whatever. When did you decide? Well, we've been discussing it—Negotiating, you mean. She lightly rubbed the tip of her nose like she was too precious to actually scratch it. We've been discussing it ever since we got married, but the timing wasn't right. I wanted to just be married for a while. I folded my arms and sat back. What happened to you? What? I paused and decided a little café was not the place for *that* conversation. I said, What happened to the no-marriage and no-kids decision we made? She looked out of the window and shrugged again. Are you feeling pressured? She laughed at me, and I hoped it was forced, but it looked and sounded real. Then I tilted my head at her. What *had* happened to our belief that marriage was a system designed to give women yet another subservient role under the guise of love and other temporary emotions? What happened to our agreement that the pressure to 'have a family' was one of the founding pillars of capitalism: to spend money on a wedding, a honeymoon, a new house, a new nursery, new baby clothes, a new car to ferry all the children around, and an annual family holiday – not to mention a new personality to fit in with all your new married-with-children friends. What happened to laughing at people who were so desperate to get married and have children because we knew that everything they were striving for was based on an idea of *happiness* that was created by advertising firms?

Was she losing herself to that man?

We're only trying, she said.

*

I learned early on that my life would have to be something more than achievements, whether academic, professional or otherwise. The measurements of success – and as a result, the approval and praise from my parents – were always rigged in my brothers' favour. The fact of their existence and genitalia usurped anything and everything I did. I could have ended world hunger and poverty, saved the planet from climate disaster and negotiated world peace, and my brother's new BMW would still best me. I learned that although a pat on the back, a hug, or your SATs results being pinned to the fridge for a week was a good feeling, it wasn't one that lasted, and that none of your greatest feats would mean anything to your relatives, who cared more that you were working hard to learn how to make jollof, suya, pounded yam and efo in order to guarantee a happy husband later in life.

It took time to learn, though. When you're young and know almost nothing about the world, your parents' opinions of you mean everything. Their rules might irritate you and inhibit your ability to have 'fun', but you still yearn for their acceptance and approval and praise, and for a while, that's what I wanted. But over the years it became clear that I was better than both of my very average and in every way ordinary older brothers: my grades were better, my room was tidier, my university prospects more prestigious, my ability to hold intelligent conversation was existent. Yet my parents were always more interested in the mundane activities of my brothers – their useless opinions and uncomfortable lack of intellect. For years I tried to find a solution, something to replace my parents' lack of interest in my life, but I never could, until that year spent with my aunt, watching her move about the world as if only she existed and only her opinion mattered. It was then I realised that if I ever wanted to be satisfied with life, I had to create success metrics of my own. And thus, BMFM was born. The key to life, with its limits and accountability, and grandiose and unattainable expectations. The key to realising that gender equality was a myth and was probably a concept invented by a man who discovered that women were in fact superior and needed to find a way to keep them in check while convincing them that equality wasn't far off.

Now everything I do is purely for my own pleasure, my own betterment, my own success. Metrics of which only I control. People's opinions of me and my actions don't even enter my thoughts, let alone affect my emotions and how I see myself. The freedom that comes with it is indescribable. Every morning I look in the mirror and say, You, yes you. I don't need to point because I'm already aware that it could only ever be about me.

When I saw my friend wander the corridors of our school, looking for ways to disappear, I saw myself in her: once unsure, now confident; once quiet, now with a clarity of voice. I saw the potential for her to become someone who walked taller, was aware of her own supremacy. I saw the opportunity to share my wealth of knowledge, of experience, and deliver the same fulfilment to someone else. For a long time it was just about me, but after meeting my friend I realised that it could be about *us*. Just the two of us.

*

We've stayed in the kitchen since we finished eating. We're nearly at the bottom of a rosé that tastes like Petit Filous, and my friend's husband has been drinking a little of his whisky every now and again. So, marriage, I say to break the silence, which is only punctuated with wine glasses being picked up and put down. My friend laughs as she drinks. What? I gesticulate between the two of them. Well, you know, you're having a baby—Trying to, my friend quickly corrects me.

Yes, you will need to deal with that *tiny* little issue first, I say. I can see her husband roll his eyes and scoff to himself. So how are things . . . between the two of you? He shakes his head and takes his phone out of his pocket. My friend looks towards him for a moment, to her wine glass, of which she twirls the stem, then looks at me. We're good, she says, and takes a sip from her glass. That's good. Would be difficult to bring a child into a negative environment, you know? My friend nods. Children are so perceptive. They know when an atmosphere isn't quite right, when people are unhappy, when they aren't quite themselves? They can sense the disingenuousness, don't you think? Mmm, she nods, another sip. I lean forward to look at her husband more clearly. What do you think? I say, my voice slightly raised as if he's far away. From where I'm sitting it seems like he's either checking scores on a betting app or playing Candy Crush. He doesn't look up and so I repeat myself. He puts his phone facedown on the table then, and looks at me, eyes half-open. Sure, children are perceptive. Absolutely, I say, picking up my glass. They can sense when people are insecure or scared. I tap the table with my nail to recapture his attention because he is picking up his phone again. Anyway, what do you think you'll be like as a parent? He shakes his head but answers quickly: I'll be fine. That's good. That's good that you think that, I say. Fake it till you make it and all that. He smiles one of those tight yeah, all right, okay smiles.

Timing is everything.

What do you think your sister will be like as a parent? I ask. He looks confused. What a strange question. Not really: she's pregnant, so reasons that you would wonder what she'll be like. My friend follows my gaze to her husband, who is still trying to compute my words, and after some struggle, he looks at my friend for confirmation. Quietly, she says, She called us earlier to tell us, said she would call you afterwards. Did you not—No, he says. One missed call but no text message, and you know she calls all the time because she's bored out there. Yikes, I say, I found out *your* sister was pregnant before *you* did. My friend pats her husband's arm and he moves it away. Says under his breath, Why didn't you tell me? I told you, she says, she asked us not to say anything because she wanted to tell you herself. Yeah, he says, downing the rest of his glass and swallowing twice to clear his mouth of the taste. But instead your friend told me. Look, I interject, neither of us could have known that she hadn't said anything. Also, you know, I say, tapping my finger on the table again, when was the last time I told you any good news? I would cherish this moment if I were you. He stands up then and says he's going upstairs to get his whisky, forgetting that he already brought the bottle down and left it on the counter by the sink. My friend's gaze follows him as he leaves the kitchen. I pat her hand to get her attention. Are you sure everything is okay with you two? She looks into her wine glass before answering. Yeah, yeah it's fine. It's just – difficult because we've been, you know, trying. She pauses and I picture the half-empty bottle of prenatal vitamins in her bathroom cupboard and try to conjure an image of her pouring them into the toilet bowl. She sighs dramatically as she pulls non-existent fibres from her trousers. I know how difficult he's finding it with both of my sisters already having kids and now his sister, too. I think he just feels like we're a bit behind, you know? I squeeze her hand sympathetically. Don't even worry about it, I say, what's meant to be will be. Her husband returns then, half-wheezing like he's out of breath, and asks where I've hidden his whisky. What do you mean? I say. I mean where is it, the whisky, where did you put it? I don't recall drinking any whisky this evening. I'm not asking if you drink whisky, I'm asking where it is. My friend turns to face me and laughs silently, putting a finger over her lips as she pulls her chair nearer to the table. He walks towards me and I lean away from him, a hand on my chest. Before you come any closer this is my personal space and I would like to make you aware of the fact that you left your precious whisky by the sink. He stops and turns towards the doorway as he clears his throat, so I speak loudly: But MAYBE. Maybe what? he says. Maybe you should slow down on the—I make a drinking gesture. Your eyes are a little . . . red. He considers my friendly advice for a moment and then leaves the room. I don't care enough to assume where he goes, but my friend rubs at her temple as though concerned. He'll be fine, I say and my friend nods. It's just—Well. I don't – I don't know. I lower my gaze to her: Please finish a sentence. Sorry, she says, and this time pinches at the bridge of her nose. I think he's just a bit stressed about the whole baby thing. *Pourquoi?* Well, you know we've been trying for a while now—A month? I interrupt her for clarity purposes. What? You've been trying for a month, right? She nods three times and pulls her hand from her nose, unaware of what she wants to do with it next: first she tries under her chin, then on top of her arm resting on the table, then crossing her arms, then she shoves both hands between her thighs and eventually decides that they feel most natural around the stem of her wine glass. Yes. We've been trying for a month. She stares at the bottom of her glass as I bore into her skull. Yeah, so if it's only been a month, he just needs to be patient, doesn't he? She nods once this time, and doesn't bring her head back up until her husband returns to the room, gets the whisky, brings it back to the table and places it next to his wine glass. I can see my friend rubbing his knee from the corner of my eye, soothing him like he's a baby, and catch a glimpse of him putting his hand on top of hers. I finish off the wine in my glass and immediately feel a head-ache coming on.

*

Once my friend's husband and I disagreed – or argued lightly – about whether or not the TV show *Scandal* was realistic. He was adamant that it was entirely unrealistic and far from any plausible truth. He was gesticulating a lot, leaning forward to look at me to make sure that I was paying attention to what he was saying. I looked at my nails while he went on and on about how it was more likely that aliens existed than an organisation like B613 that routinely carried out assassinations or hits. When he'd finally finished, I countered that we know almost nothing about the day-to-day operations of the government and referred to a politics class my friend and I took at school. I asked my friend to confirm what I was saying. She nodded and then looked at her husband for where the conversation would go next. He started to speak but I pressed my friend for a verbal confirmation. Tell him what our teacher said about the percentage of what we really know, what was it again? Umm, she said, and then paused for a few seconds. I can't remember. Really? I said. She nodded and turned back to her husband, who looked at me, somewhat confused, then back to his wife, and took the silence as his cue to continue.

I think about that day sometimes when I watch my friend with her husband. I realise it was the beginning of her reversion into the person she was before me. I found reasons to explain it away the first time. But then it happened again, and again, during nights when I'd come over and her husband would be around. She would sit and look between the two of us, laugh quietly instead of loudly like she used to, refuse to take a side in an argument where she used to be irritated by people who insisted on staying on the fence. After she went to university she would talk all the time, about anything, bring up topics that intrigued or annoyed her, deliver unsolicited opinions about other people with such cutting accuracy that even I was impressed. Now, she's different. She lets everything pass by her and through her. It seems like she has no capacity or interest for participation any more.

But then again, our friendship has remained the same in many ways. The drinks, the time spent together, the days and nights out, the shopping, the gossiping, the exchanging of stories. Except for the fact that the stories and gossip are all mine, and the time spent together must be factored around the hours in which her husband demands hers. Time she willingly gives to him without complaint or protest – for example, our annual holiday, that we should have been on . . . today. The whole thing is like a weird little transaction where my card always gets declined and his has no credit limit. These days, she says, Could you do next week? when I suggest plans to meet for dinner, or, We're going to [insert generic expensive restaurant or romantic date activity here] that day. Really? I'll ask, and she'll nod and shrug, say, It's nice.

The pursuit of the life we talked about – the one in which

we live selfishly, do everything in the service of ourselves –
seems to have evaporated into nothing, or into a watered-
down version of whatever this is. I hoped and thought that
this thing with the husband was just a phase. That marriage,
and then later the notoriety of divorce, would be yet another
life experience that would separate the two of us from everyone else, pursuing ideals created for them by someone else.

But it's clear that something more significant has shifted
in my friend since I've been away. Whether it's pressure from
her in-laws or from the man who sleeps in her bed I'm not
sure, but what I do know is that *this* life – the one with children and PTA meetings and school drop-offs and describing
three-year-olds as being thirty-six months – is a life that she
is dangerously close to living. She is standing on the edge
with her hands at her back, her husband behind her, ready
to push. So what kind of friend would I be if I let him?

*

It's partly my fault, I introduced her to him, I even gave his
sister her number, but I thought she would have her fun with
him, he would fall in love with her, and then she would aban-
don him like excessive Amazon packaging. But she liked
him, or so she said, and she kept him around. I have tried
for years now, as in literally four years, to understand what
it is she likes about this particular breed, and I can't figure it

out. He has an average face, yes, and he has a good job; his sister is interesting so in a way his genes are acceptable, but he has no personality. He works in tech or something, which is universal code for 'I have no personality'. He dresses like he models for Zara, which not even the people who model for Zara do, and he every now and again calls me 'Ma' in the thickest Yoruba accent he can put on, which he thinks annoys me but only reaffirms the inexplicable mystery of his existence in my friend's, and therefore my, life.

When I first met him, I thought he was mildly interesting. He was, and remains, about six foot, despite what he tells others, casually, in conversation, completely unprovoked. I thought he was harmless. He had a pretentiousness about him that convinced me that he wouldn't last, that his generic face would lose its lustre for my friend around the two-week mark. So I was of course disappointed when my friend/sister/partner/rib/extension-of-self told me that she was going to go on a date with the human equivalent of a Bic pen. And then I was deeply distressed and entirely confounded when she said she was going to marry him. I tried, as much as I could, to convince her not to, to show her that he didn't fit into our plans, share our humour, our shorthand. He would not appreciate that we were trying to avoid becoming our mothers. He couldn't comprehend the journey she'd been on, and how long it had taken her to unlearn the personality that her parents had painted on to her. It was safe, this man, this marriage, but I knew she was more than that. More than the too-tight cardigans and overexposed ankles; more than a man with nothing to offer except for a barely decent amount of facial hair and an inoffensive monthly pay cheque. And yet for reasons even advanced medicine cannot explain, she actually seems to like him. Sometimes when we're together and he calls her, she smiles when she sees his name on her phone and I question how loudly I should retch to make my point, but my therapist tells me that I am projecting, so I've let my friend be. I've let a man who has never watched a single episode of *Law & Order: SVU* drag my friend from life to death-of-self and away from every-thing we spent years planning. But after the little procrea-tion revelation I found today in the bathroom, it has become exceedingly clear that I've let her be for too long, and that if I don't do something now, I will have to learn to describe our friendship in past tense.

*

I pictured our friendship like this: a shared wine cellar the size of a modest studio flat, holidays in Greece and Singa-pore. Weekend trips to Sicily, Paris, Amsterdam and Berlin. Christmases on Victoria Island in Lagos. Homes within walking distance of one another. I love her, but boundaries are important and having my own space is worth more than any person I know. Discussions about the last *New Yorker* article we read or the latest *Guardian* write-up about the top ten Beyoncé songs and our confusion when we discover that her timeless classics are missing. Long walks in all the decent parks that are not overrun with crying children and tired parents, or adolescents who like smoking ground-up kale and drinking WKD. Meanderings around art galleries where we bump into moderately famous people who compliment our coats and our shoes and invite us to gatherings with other moderately famous and marginally interesting people.

I pictured the two of us thriving, attending the weddings of family and friends and smugly responding to enquiries about our marital and fertility statuses with the number of digits in our bank balances and the anti-gravitational pull of our upper bodies in comparison to our married and mothering counterparts. I pictured continued wealth and success with minimal effort required. I pictured shared experiences, ideas and hopes for the future; I pictured us more than content, bonded for life by an unceasing desire not to be tied down by anyone else, a pursuit of freedom and independence entirely on our own terms.

I knew what freedom was like because of the gap year I took after my A levels. I didn't want to mope around my first year of university, unable to drink and begging the three other Black girls in my halls to use their ID, only to be both pleased and offended when I would be let in to a venue using a photo that looked nothing like me. So I went to San Francisco to intern at a law firm where my aunt – the allegedly lonely single one – worked, and stayed with her in her penthouse. She was divorced with a son who went to a faraway boarding school and lived as though she had no responsibilities. She took me to art galleries, painting classes and film screenings, and let me sit in on meetings with her clients. She took me to her holiday home in Mexico, somehow got us into Cuba using her work connections, and took me shopping in Miami. Some days when she woke up and didn't want to work, she would email her assistant and say she was taking a personal day and to move all of her meetings, then she would ask me what I wanted to do and I could name an activity in a different state and she would make it happen. She opened my eyes entirely to the idea that living for yourself was the only way to even come close to being satisfied.

I invited my friend to stay with me in San Francisco over the summer holiday that year but her parents said no, that she'd be working towards her A levels and studying all summer, taking part in activities that would boost her applications and eligibility for her top university choices, UCL and LSE. She spent that summer toiling away at her desk and participating in various uninteresting extracurricular enterprises at her parents' behest. Meanwhile, I, already accepted to Cambridge, spent the summer with my aunt, living as though my life in England was something of the past.

When I returned briefly for Christmas that year my friend came over, sat on my bed as I unpacked, and asked what it was like. I had already shown her the photos of me on the beach, at restaurants, in Cuba, in Mexico, standing in front of the Hollywood sign in LA, so I turned to her, an overworn swimsuit in my hand. What do you mean? Like, not being here, having to work, to study, what is it like? I dropped the swimsuit into the laundry basket. Stop doing everything your parents say and you'll see for yourself, I said. And for a while, a long time in fact, she did. At university we would Skype and she'd tell me about how good it felt not to return home to a select committee inquiry about her whereabouts, activities, actions and attitude that day. That she loved waking up to the sound of her flatmates arguing in the kitchen or dealing with the fire alarm going off every time her flatmate forgot to open the window when he smoked in his room. That she found a hilarious kind of thrill in being asked about herself and making up weird little stories about being from a place she had never even visited or being an only child. That it was extremely enjoyable to be able to talk back when someone much older said something incorrect or barely coherent and not worry about receiving an hour-long lecture on respect. That being able to stand up for herself was one of the most liberating things she had ever done. This is what I was talking about, I would tell her. And she would nod, smiling, a canned pina colada in hand, I get it now.

We were already close by the time we went to university, but her experience, her reawakening, or her rebirth as she likes to call it, brought us even closer. We could finally share stories that were eye-opening or embarrassing or educational. She was no longer just listening to me recount tales from a life she thought was impossible to achieve. We found a new kind of intimacy to our friendship that became a sisterhood. A bond that went beyond blood and kindness and interest as an obligation – we were committed to each other and to keeping each other accountable to the ideals that we shared. We cultivated a trust that few romantic relationships can claim to possess, and we knew that we had something worth protecting, no matter the cost.

So it falls upon me, the one between the two of us who still has her eyes open, to do the protecting and reminding. To remind her of the plans we made when we began our adult lives, and to hold on to the hope that we'll laugh about all of this one day over a bottle of wine.

*

My friend's husband goes into the living room to take a call from his mother, and when he returns my friend and

I are discussing the bets I made with our siblings and various family members about how long their relationship will last. She has since drunk part of her husband's glass of the yoghurt-tasting rosé and her energy has returned. She laughs as I reel off the list of bets: Well, my oldest brother said twelve years – he says after you have a couple of kids you'll realise your parenting styles are different and go your separate ways. Said you'll file first, I nod towards my friend. Oooh, she says, eager to hear everything. Your oldest sister said you'd go the distance at first, but then I told her about how I convinced you to cancel your first date and she said eight years. I don't look over at my friend's husband, but out of the corner of my eye I can see him shake his head as he goes to get a whisky glass from the cupboard and fills it with some ice from the freezer. Ha, my friend says, and tries to stifle the rest of her laughter. I go through the other votes by counting them on my fingers and wait until my friend's husband sits back at the table, angled slightly away from us, before I get to mine.

Well, I say, pretending to be coy, I said two and a half years, so I've already lost. What? Only two and a half years? I wince at my friend to indicate that her husband doesn't find our topic of conversation as riveting as I do. Your lovely husband and I didn't really get on during the wedding planning period, and given how close you and I are . . . I thought if that didn't work itself out – he and I, I mean – things between you two might have got a little . . . uncomfortable. My friend considers my reasoning and nods her head, her mouth in a thoughtful line.

Her husband smiles as he struggles with the glass topper on the bottle of whisky. You're very confident to assume that your friendship would be more important than our marriage, don't you think? What do you mean? I say, putting my chin in my hand and resting my elbow on the table as if curious and aloof. He shakes his head, and with the bottle finally open, pours himself a generous glass. I think it's great that you've exceeded my expectations, don't you? My friend and I toast as her husband shakes his head again, then lifts his glass towards his mouth as he points at me. Your expectations aren't really anything to be held in any kind of esteem, though, are they? Why's that? Because they're from someone who is in denial about their own singleness. My friend starts fiddling with her rings and I sit up. I thought it would take a little longer for him to start glitching but he's started early so I bite. Who says I'm in denial? He shakes his head yet again and I lean forward more, take a small sip of my wine and place the glass down firmly. Oh, you know. No, no I don't, please do inform me about my denial, I'm intrigued. Well, he says, taking a dramatic pause to sip from his glass again, you have only one friend left on planet Earth who can stand to be around you – he indicates towards my friend – you are so lonely that you spend ninety-five per cent of your waking hours at our house because you can't bear spending time alone, and of course, you're still bitter about that . . . thing. I'm making that face people make just before they laugh, where you can see the laughter in their cheeks, and my friend is running her fingers along the patterns of the marble table in order to avoid making eye contact with either of us. Her husband watches me open my mouth like I'm about to speak, but I lift my wine glass to my mouth instead. I tip my head back further than normal to drink it and maintain eye contact with him as I do. The sound of my wine glass touching the table echoes as I put it down and my friend and her husband are looking at me when I finally speak. Bitter about what? He cocks his head to one side with his mouth slightly open, smiling. Come on. You *know*. I shake my head and shrug my shoulders, oozing nonchalance. No, really, honestly, I don't. Tell me. He purses his lips and shrugs, and I can tell from here that his eyes are a little red at the edges. He finally says: Well my wife did kiss that boy you liked, didn't she?

*

I have tried almost everything to remind my friend of what awaits her on the other side of marriage. To take her back to the day we sat in her room at university drinking Desperados with limes stuck in the necks of the bottles and mapped out the rest of our lives. The places we would visit, the people we would meet, the way we would behave, the things we would buy, the exact phrases we would say to our parents and siblings when they asked us for updates, the looks we would attract when we showed up to family gatherings, the text messages we would screenshot from men trying to garner our interest, the clothes we would wear to our secondary-school reunions, the places we would go for food afterwards for the debrief. I have tried over dinners, during holidays, at events, on phone calls. And sometimes I think I can feel her peeling this strange new layer of 'wife' off and returning to the woman I know. I had hoped that our annual holiday would have been the perfect opportunity to nurture the revision, make it official in some way – maybe we'd sign a legally binding document over martinis and oysters. But every day the time I have to convince her is limited by missed dinners, rescheduled holidays and unanswered phone calls, and lately I see her behaving more and more like a wife, stroking the back of his neck while we're watching a film, offering to get him a cup of tea or refill his wine glass. Offering to have his children. She rarely initiates jokes about marriage or laughs at people who are married any more, has 'Wife, Daughter, Friend' as her Instagram bio and collects cookery books even though she never cooks. Instead she laughs at her husband's feeble attempts at humour, and when she says 'we' she is usually referring to herself and her husband, not the two of us. Maybe I'm being melodramatic, but people don't take pregnancy tests for fun, and prenatal vitamins are advanced but I can't name a single non-pregnant person who has ever taken them just for the health benefits. So it's down to this: she either wants our life or she doesn't.

*

My friend looks at me, blinks twice. I roll my eyes and twist the wine glass between my fingers at the stem. It's important that her husband believes this moment doesn't bother me, because it is his life's work to do so. You knew? she says. I know everything, I say nonchalantly, I just don't *care* about everything. Secrets, secrets, her husband says, smirking like he just told a complex joke that was well received. My friend is still looking at me, like she wants to apologise. Oh no, you don't need to look like that, I say quickly, I really, really don't care. She nods slowly, and it's uncomfortable how pleadingly she looks at me as she sips the last of her wine. She is realising that I know there are two kinds of intimacy in her life, and I know exactly where she has ranked ours. She readjusts her wedding and engagement rings again, making sure they're centred, before fixing a new smile on her face. Are you still hungry? I am but my reply sounds perfectly balanced: No, I'm all right, thanks. You sure? she counters, standing up. I'm sure we have some more snacks hidden here somewhere, right? She looks to her husband, who like me is no longer interested in light, purposeless exchanges. Or didn't we get, like, prawn crackers with our order? She looks around the table for the empty bag. OR, she says at a higher volume, maybe we can order some more food? She looks between us and waits for an answer. I pat the seat behind her. Sit down, we're fine. I stare into the liquid of my glass and look at my reflection. Eventually, I've had enough of the waiting. Drinking games? I suggest. Neither of them speaks for a few seconds, and then my friend finally does: More wine?

My friend goes to get another bottle from the wine cooler. While she crouches down carefully, steadying herself against a cupboard door to deliberate, her husband leans towards me slightly and half-whispers, You know, if *she* couldn't even tell you about the boy from school – his intonation rises like he's asking me a question – I mean, what else don't you guys know about each other? I consider responding before he continues his whisky-fuelled monologue. I think, he says, pinching the tip of his nose briefly, that she's a bit tired of you, like there are just things she doesn't want to tell you because you're so . . . so embedded in her life. You are all the way inside her life and she wants to keep some things to herself, but you just won't leave her alone. The last month without you was pure bliss for her, she could finally breathe without you constantly hovering. I push my glass away, rest my elbows on the table and place my chin in my hands so he can recite his tell-all to me knowing that I am focused on our conversation. He readjusts himself in his seat and continues. Did she tell you, for example, that we're turning one of the upstairs rooms into a nursery? Or that she hates it when you smoke in the house? Did you notice that we don't have ash-trays around for you any more? I mean – he pauses to shuffle closer and then lowers his voice further: You just have to consider, he says, that life, and people, move on, grow up, advance, and that your version of life, the stagnant, self-deluding thing that it is, hasn't got a place in hers any more. That you don't know her any more. The things she doesn't tell you? She tells me instead. We have something tangible and invaluable between us. He leans back into his seat and narrows his eyes at me in a weird-looking squint. Trust. Do you even know what that is? Then he shrugs with his lips pulled into a line. I don't turn my head to look at him because energy is a valuable resource, but I let my eyes drift to the side as he crosses his arms, satisfied with himself.

My friend returns a few seconds later with a bottle of red and struggles with the cork. She finally gets it open and takes her time pouring each of our glasses. She makes a point of doing mine first and filling it more than is necessary. I flash a tight smile of thanks and she flashes one back and then pours her own. We settle into silence again and then the two of them start talking about something to do with the house, and my friend angles herself slightly away from me in order to face her husband. So, I say eventually. Your husband says you and I aren't completely honest with each other. She looks at her husband first before she turns to face me – What?

*

There was a time, maybe two years ago, when I really did think they might be on the brink. He got a new job and of course it paid well, but he was working a lot, rarely home, a little irritable. Over drinks one day my friend told me that they were barely having sex, that she was spending a lot of time alone scrolling mindlessly through Instagram for ways to entertain herself because he was never around, and in a moment of weakness in which I made it seem as though I cared about the success of her marriage, I asked if she'd spoken to him about it, and she said no. She said she didn't want to make things worse for him because he was already stressed. I looked behind her, behind myself, up at the ceiling, and put a hand against my forehead like I was looking for someone lost at sea and she asked what I was doing. Trying to locate your backbone, I said. She laughed, but I was concerned. This was the woman who, after a number of drinks, had once flicked black liquid eyeliner at an ex-boyfriend – who was wearing a crisp white shirt – because he'd not wished her happy birthday. Sitting in front of me that day was some diluted version of that woman, shrinking herself for the convenience of a man. Little has changed since then.

So I've decided to change tactics. If she can't see that she's not herself, then there's someone else who will. Someone who has been waiting three years to have a baby and whose patience, like mine, is wearing thin.

I've seen the way he looks at her when I tell stories about the life we had together before he existed, or the way he waits for her to defend him and tell me to stop when I make a dig about his hair or his clothes or how he walks. Once when we were watching a period drama on TV, his wife, three glasses of wine and two very strong gin and tonics in, said that men hadn't changed at all and still expected women to do everything, and I watched as his mouth made its way into a frown and his eyes drifted to glance over at her. He sees what I see, but from the other side. A woman in between two selves, undecided as to which she can remain loyal. Where I see uncomfortable levels of domesticity and submission, he sees impolite outspokenness and levels of negative emotion rarely observed. What he thinks is a new person emerging in short and sometimes alcohol-fuelled bursts, I know is the occasional reappearance of my misguided friend. We are trying to solve the same problem, but our judgements on the solution differ significantly.

*

I should have known that exposing the cracks in the veneer my friend has created for her husband was never going to be easy. I've had to wait for the right moment, in part because he works very hard not to listen to anything I say. Makes a point of either leaving the room, scrolling through his phone or doing something noisy in the background to block out the sound of my voice. So only today, sat listening to her husband spin his sentimental web about trust and the like, did I realise what I could do and how I could do it. I'm almost embarrassed to admit that idea has been staring me in the face for years. A student's greatest nightmare. A tale as old as time: Shakespeare. People blame the messenger for not getting to Romeo in time, or Romeo for acting rashly, but the true culprit is Balthasar. Not because he means to incite a double suicide, but because he sows seeds of doubt. The very suggestion that Juliet might not be alive convinces Romeo of the fact without really interrogating it, and from there, everything else falls apart. Like I said, all good things come to an end, and a marriage, in which the affection is more transactional than romantic, is unlikely to hold much real trust within it. Besides, everybody sees what they want to in the end, no matter how far-fetched. A woman who finds a foreign smell or hair or mark on her husband's clothing will believe he's having an affair the moment she finds it, because doubt tells her it's true. You will go back and check you've turned the oven off after you've already got into your car because doubt will tell you otherwise. Doubt and truth are so close that it's sometimes impossible to tell them apart.

*

But I disagree, I say to my friend. I think we're honest with each other about everything. A schoolboy kiss is hardly a revelation. At this her mouth opens slightly, and she turns back to look at her husband. Why would you say that? He sighs and takes a long sip of his whisky, wipes his finger along the edge of the glass where some of it has dripped down and licks his finger. Well, I think if you never talked about it after all these years, what else might you not have talked about? It's not an indictment on your friendship, just an observation. Every relationship has secrets. I nod dramatically. Being yourself, I say, being true to yourself, and then of course being honest and upfront is absolutely key to any relationship. Without that, what are we? Anything built on a lie or secrets isn't going to last. The foundations will never be strong enough to carry the weight of an untruth for very long. My friend's husband has his brow creased in confusion. Yes, he says slowly, shocked by his own agreement with me. I nod at him and turn back to my friend and put my hand over hers on the table. That's why I think you should tell him.

After a moment my friend's husband leans forward to gauge his wife's reaction, and I can see that their facial expressions are the same: bewildered. Tell him what? I shake my head. Oh, you probably already told him, that's why you're drinking, I see it now! Ugh, I didn't even make the connection. My friend turns her head slightly as her confusion grows. Tell him what? she says again. Tell him what? her husband repeats. What are you talking about? my friend says, one hand on her wine glass. About, you know – I feign an attempt to whisper while pointing my head slightly in the direction of the corridor. My friend's husband follows my head movement and walks out to the corridor to inspect its every inch. I have to control my face as I watch him do this because my friend is still looking at me, waiting for an answer. What are you talking about? she mouths, and switches over our hands so hers are on top of mine, and she squeezes the centre of my hand lightly. Just tell him, I think he'll get it, I say at a normal volume as her husband comes back into the kitchen, looking out of breath. He remains standing. Look, maybe you should sit down – an attempt at empathy. My friend lowers her head further, then squeezes my hand again, lighter than last time so that her husband is less likely to notice. He loves you, he won't be upset. I put an emphasis on the words 'won't' and 'upset' and my friend brings her head back up, exhales impatiently and shakes her head as she removes her hand from mine. Upset about what? Her husband has reluctantly sat down now, but I can tell from his jerky movements that he's bouncing his leg up and down under the table. No one says anything for a few moments, and suddenly he lifts his glass and downs the rest of his whisky, about half the glass. This is stupid, my friend says, and her husband says, If it's so stupid then just tell me. There is nothing to tell you, she says, she's just drunk.

I watch him as he looks past his wife and towards me, and I notice that his eyes are even redder than they were before. D'you want some water? I ask, moving my head so that he can see my whole face behind his wife's. No. He lifts his hand a little like he might slam it on the table, and instead looks to his wife and says, Just tell me. She's right, I won't be upset.

Babe, she says, picking up his lifted hand and putting it in hers. I honestly don't know what she's talking abou—

The back and forth is starting to bore me so I interject. Oh for goodness' sake just tell him you switched out your vitamins for birth control.

I'm not sure if my friend turns around slowly or if I see her turn in slow motion, but either way it's a marvel to witness because her expression is both desperate and angry at the same time. He was bound to figure it out. You and I have drunk a *lot* today. I've been gone for a month and you're still not pregnant. Surely he's realised you're not getting pregnant despite all the trying you're doing? I say the last part bluntly, like it's a rhetorical question, and drink some of my wine so my words both echo and disappear into the glass at the same time. This isn't funny, my friend says, and then turns back to her husband. You can't joke about this – it's serious, her husband says, and I flare my eyes wide, suddenly incensed by the accusation. Excuse me, I say, hand on my chest, I don't joke about serious issues like this.

In my wildest dreams red steam comes out of his ears and nose, but in reality he exhales loudly and looks at his wife, who is now tugging at the bottom of his T-shirt. You know I would not do that, she says. We agreed one child so I said let's try for one child. I don't lie, you know me. He remains quiet, just looking at her for a few seconds and then begins to speak, but in her desperation she doubles down – Why would I bother swapping out the pills when I could just say no? He looks past his wife and at me, and I continue sipping from my wine glass. I can almost read verbatim what he's thinking when he turns back to his wife and says: Why can't I believe you?

I touch my friend's shoulder lightly and she immediately shrugs me off. I did say that you should have just been honest about it from the start. Saves everyone a lot of—Come on, she says to her husband, whose eyes are flitting between the two of us. In these moments of fragility I can tell that he is wondering who to believe – the woman who always says what she thinks, or the woman who rarely says anything at all.

Look, why don't you just go and check the cupboard in the bathroom where she keeps them and have a look for yourself. Maybe I'm wrong, maybe she's stopped swapping them out, but to just put this whole thing to bed, I would say go and have a look. See what colour they are or whatever. Temi, why are you doing this? my friend says without turning around. Her fingers lose their grip on the bottom of his T-shirt as he stands up. Can you just stop for a second. Do you genuinely believe *her* over me? She stands too, looking up at him, and he looks down at her, then again past her and to me. Back and forth. Back and forth.

You did take some convincing, he says, and my friend looks like she's on the verge of a tantrum. Why on earth would I swap out my pills then? I'd just tell you I don't want a baby. You've watched me take my birth control every morning for years. You know what those pills look like, what colour they are. He looks at her squarely now. No, I don't. I've seen you take them but I don't know what colour they are. Really? Really. In all the years I've taken them you've never noticed the colour of them? I can't remember what they look like. My friend tries to calm her increasing frustration and swaps her intensity for reason instead. Fine, but if you're seriously going to accuse me of something like this, can you be honest with yourself, and at least admit that the only reason, the *only* reason you can't say for sure is because of her. Is because she – she points at me without turning – said that I swapped them? He takes one last look at me, and I've anticipated this, so I'm looking directly at him, eyes still, when he does. Can you tell me the colour of your vitamins? he says. It's a few seconds before I hear my friend exhale, and I lift my glass from the table, swirl the remaining wine in it around a few times before swallowing the rest in a single gulp, and set the glass back down on the table. Quietly this time.

She brings a hand to her hip like she's supporting her back and says, No, but can you? A chalky-yellow colour, he responds quickly, and she drops her shoulders, exasperated. I reach for the wine bottle in the middle of the table just as he turns to head for the bathroom, and she catches his hand.

Wait, she says.

In the sink are a bowl and a plate, a stray noodle trapped in the teeth of the fork left to one side. Three empty wine bottles sit by the recycling box, two other empty bottles on the table, one half-empty bottle of red in the middle, its cork lying neatly next to it. The white bags in which the Japanese food came sit crumpled by one of the cupboards, with the empty food containers stuffed into the overfull bin next to the door to the garden. There are three wine glasses on the table, all of them empty, and a whisky glass with ice still melting inside. A few crisp crumbs from earlier in the afternoon are sprinkled by the kitchen doorway; a cork that rolled off the counter sits beside them. On the very edge of the table is the near-empty bottle of whisky owned by a man who is standing with his hands by his sides, looking at his wife, trying to recognise her. She is standing opposite him, her eyes desperate to communicate honesty, and failing. And behind them both is a woman, pouring herself another glass of wine.

Acknowledgements

First, thank you to my parents – for the existence, for the constant love, support and enthusiasm. For never telling me to try something different, for trusting me, and for essentially dragging me to the library every week as a child and forcing me to read. Without you, there absolutely would not be a book at all, because there never would have been a reader. These few lines aren't enough to thank you for everything you've done. I love you immeasurably and I am so grateful for you.

To my sister, my best friend, my favourite person in the world, thank you for being the best person I know, for always being there and for being excited about essentially everything I've ever written, even the things I didn't let you read because they were horrific. Thank you for dipping your toe back into the fiction pool just for me! To Rob, my broseph from another Joseph, thank you for being *so* hyped about this whole process, for your support and excitement, and for understanding when I was referencing books and the rest of the family had no idea what I was talking about!

Grace, my rib, my right hand *everything*, how boring I would be without you. To just say thank you even sounds a little ridiculous considering the *huge* role you played in this book existing. From *that* conversation to being the first person to read it and telling me it was funny (you should never have done that, have you seen the size of my head lately?), to crying with me (tears of joy) on FaceTime when it all came together, this book is a real thing because of your belief and encouragement. I am so unbelievably blessed by your sisterhood.

To my friends who are more like family, and actual family who kept me on track and gave me deadlines(!) (thank you Aunty Abiola Shutti – without you I may not have actually finished this book!!), who told me to stop scrolling through TikTok when I should have been writing (Christina Shutti), who helped me organise my chaotic schedule in order to make time for edits (Queen of Life Sabah Khan), who sat with me on FaceTime whilst I procrastinated or tried to figure out timelines and were *brutally* honest about some proposed jokes that have since been cut . . . (Ammara Isa, Haya Junaid, Eden McKenzie-Goddard), who sent me every Twitter mention and Instagram post (and have been my walking pitch, general sounding board and all-time greatest hype man,

Ammara Isa, again), who have zero clue about how publishing works but have been so excited for me ever since you heard I'd written a book (Juwon Bajomo, Itunu Para-Mallam, Tolu Kupoluyi, Bisi and Tobi Oduntan).

To the Uncles and Aunties who have been supportive of everything I've done since I was born and who have showered me with love and encouragement every day of my life, with particular shoutouts to Aunty Yinka Omorogbe, and Uncle Kayode and Aunty Yetunde Onifade, my bonus/second parents whose unconditional love and support have been a constant presence.

To the friends who have been shouting me out and supporting and posting/tweeting/retweeting, sending messages of support and just been generally fantastic, I could write a *lot* about how privileged I am to have you in my life, but if I did we'd have to add about sixteen extra pages, but please know that your part in this whole process is invaluable and I am forever grateful for you: Georgina Ugen, Bengono Bessala Nyada De Besbeck, Nancy Adimora, Liv Chant, Jack Dillon, Holly Ashenden, Marianne Tatepo, Lucy Stewart & Margot Gray (always keeping me humble!!), Beth Wickington (who has believed since the *other other other* book), Becca Bryant, Charlotte Cross, Charlotte Brown, Jack Renninson, Catriona Beamish, Molly Walker-Sharp, Andrew Davis, Bobby Mostyn-Owen, Iman Amrani, Haddi Ceesay, Jen Garside (and all the book club ladies!), June Eric-Udorie,

Jade Abernethy, Hattie Cooke, Jasper Dunning, Aimee Batchelor, Emily Rhodes, Lauren Sainthouse, Bryony Ball, Wei Ming Kam, Eishar Brar, Viki Cheung and Jack Borthwick.

Angelique! The first person to ever read any of my long-form writing, your enthusiasm and support helped me to make one of the best decisions I've ever made and your unwavering belief and excitement has meant everything. You are a phenomenal friend. Thank you.

To Claire Kohda and Sophie Burks, to whom I asked a ridiculous number of questions that were answered with so much grace and patience, thank you! This process would have been very different without your expertise and kindness.

To Nikesh Shukla, the man who always has time for everyone, thank you for your mentorship and generosity over the years and for somehow finding the time and energy to be the biggest supporter and advocate of everyone. You've changed so many lives and I will be forever grateful to know you.

Niki Chang, the world's greatest literary agent, fiercest advocate, brilliant editor, confidence booster, I could go on and on. There are not adequate words to describe how honoured I am to call you not only my agent but my friend. I am in awe (and actually a bit scared?) of your work ethic and how much energy you pour into everyone in your life. Thank you for being everything I wanted and everything I didn't even know I needed. I am so, so, glad that we get to do this together.

To David Evans, Nicky Lund, Sophia Rahim and everyone at David Higham Associates for your excellent expertise,
support and championing of this book and of me, thank you!

To my ingenious editors, Željka Marošević and Sally
Kim, where would I be without you both?! You are detailed-
oriented in a way I have never seen but I am very grateful for,
you are ridiculously intelligent, kind, funny, incredibly perceptive, patient, joyful and two of the most brilliant women
I know. Thank you for helping me to shape this book into
the much, much better story that it is today, for asking the
important questions and making me a better writer. Working with you both has been a dream. Thank you for making
me and this book feel so safe with you.

To the Jonathan Cape and Putnam teams who have been
so, so kind about this book but more importantly have
worked so hard on it too. From Tarini Sipahimalani, Cécile
Pin, Rowena Skelton-Wallace, Michal Shavit and Hannah
Telfer, to Chloe Healy, Katrina Northern, Helia Daryani,
Ashley McClay, Brennin Cummings, Emily Leopold and
Jazmin Miller in marketing and Lucie Cuthbertson-Twiggs,
Anna Redman Aylward, Alexis Welby, Katie McKee and
Nicole Biton in publicity, to Malissa Mistry, Nat Breakwell,
Caitlin Knight and Justin Ward-Turner in sales, Janice
Barral and Konrad Kirkham in production and Suzanne
Dean, Anna Morrison and Vi-An Nguyen in design for the
outstanding covers (you are all insanely talented), finance

and distribution, the meticulous copy-editors Madeline Hopkins and Sarah-Jane Forder, and proofreaders Saba Ahmed, Noreen McAuliffe and Meg Drislane who stopped me from embarrassing myself(!!). Every single book takes a team to bring it out into the world and your work on *The Three of Us* has been spectacular. I am extremely privileged and proud to have been able to work with all of you.

I'm almost done, I promise! To my English school teachers and university Professors (and to all English school teachers and professors), thank you for helping me to find a place at school and university where I felt most at home, and for helping me to find a love for language and make it into something special. Thank you for your patience and enthusiasm and kindness. Mrs Freed, Mrs Hammers, Mrs Spreadbury, Mrs Gale, Mrs Caligari, Dr Ranka Primorac, Prof John McGavin, I hope this book makes you proud and reminds you that what you do and have done remains incredibly important.

To all at the Black Writers' Guild, thank you for your support and for everything you work towards and work for – particularly Nels Abbey, Sharmaine Lovegrove, Symeon Brown, Derek Owusu and Elijah Lawal. To all the booksellers who have recommended or mentioned this book, put it on a shelf – thank you, your work is invaluable and your recommendations mean everything.

*

To my grandfathers and grandmother, cousin Tobi and Aunty Liz who couldn't be here to read it, I hope in some way you know that you had something to do with all of this too.

Finally – see, you made it – thank you to you, yes, *you* who are reading this, who have taken the time to read this book. I am very, very grateful that you let my imagination take up this much of your time, and even more thankful that you stayed to find out the names of all the people who made this book a possibility.